LOST ISLAND

BOOKS BY
JAMES NORMAN HALL

DOCTOR DOGBODY'S LEG

LOST ISLAND

IN COLLABORATION WITH
CHARLES NORDHOFF

FALCONS OF FRANCE

THE BOUNTY TRILOGY

THE HURRICANE

THE DARK RIVER

NO MORE GAS

BOTANY BAY

MEN WITHOUT COUNTRY

# JAMES NORMAN HALL

LOST ISLAND

AN ATLANTIC MONTHLY PRESS BOOK

LITTLE, BROWN AND COMPANY · BOSTON

1944

COPYRIGHT 1944, BY JAMES NORMAN HALL

ALL RIGHTS RESERVED, INCLUDING THE RIGHT
TO REPRODUCE THIS BOOK OR PORTIONS
THEREOF IN ANY FORM

ATLANTIC–LITTLE, BROWN BOOKS
ARE PUBLISHED BY
LITTLE, BROWN AND COMPANY
IN ASSOCIATION WITH
THE ATLANTIC MONTHLY PRESS

PRINTED IN THE UNITED STATES OF AMERICA
BY H. WOLFF, NEW YORK

To

CARL BEECHER, WALTER G. SMITH,
and J. FRANK STIMSON

LOST ISLAND

I

CHANCE, IN A BENEVOLENT mood, had consented that the pathways of three old friends and former comrades in World War I should cross for the first time in twenty years. The boon deserved to be enjoyed at leisure, and they had gone from San Francisco, the place of the unexpected meeting, across the bay to Berkeley, where Philip Marsh, Professor of History in the University of California, had his home, high up in the Berkeley hills. After dinner, Mrs. Marsh, an understanding woman, had left her husband alone for the evening with his guests, and now they were seated in the library whose great west window framed a magnificent panorama of the bay to the Golden Gate and beyond. The bridge between the heads, clearly etched at first against the afterglow, faded slowly from view until it could be seen no more.

All three men were in their middle fifties. Professor Marsh was a tall spare fellow somewhat frail in appearance, but the alert keen glance of the gray eyes was that which his friends remembered in the infantry lieutenant of a generation before. Charles Webber, a New Englander, had recently come to the West Coast to fill a post in a federal office connected with civilian defense. George Dodd, the only one of them again in uniform, was an officer of Engineers. He was sturdily built, slow of speech and slow of movement, and he had the odd habit of frequently passing his open fingers over the top of his bald head as though to ruffle the hair he had forgotten was no longer there.

Webber, slumped comfortably down in his chair, was speaking with a kind of wry humor of his share in the second phase of a world war that seemed destined never to have an end.

"A fifth wheel," he was saying; "rolling around to no conceivable purpose so far as I can see. Thousands of my kind have been set in motion from Washington, and the lot of us are not worth one of the fifth wheels clamped to the rear end of a motorcar."

"Don't be so modest, Charlie," Professor Marsh replied. "I'll bet you think no end of yourself and of what you're doing, if the truth were known."

"No," said Webber, with some heat. "Honestly, I can't see that my work has the slightest value for anyone, anywhere. It's mere busyness without a justifiable end in view. . . . George, what kind of a wheel are you, if it's fair to ask? An essential part of Juggernaut? Crushing and grinding to some purpose?"

"I'm supposed to be," Dodd replied.

"And yet you don't seem particularly happy about it."

"I didn't know that happiness was concerned here."

"Of course not," said Webber. "But satisfaction is — a kind of grim satisfaction, if one has something essential to do." He turned to Professor Marsh. "Phil, you have a try. See if you can break through this engineer's iron reserve. Have you noticed? All through dinner he edged away from any mention of his part in the war effort. Shouldn't wonder if the engineer's insignia were pure camouflage. He's probably connected with the F.B.I."

"What *are* you doing, George?" Marsh asked. "Engineers, surely, have nothing to be reticent about."

"Loafing, for this one night, at least," said Dodd. "I'm down from Alaska for a few days. I've been out there, too," he added, with a vague wave of the hand to the westward.

" 'Out there'!" said Webber. "How hard it is to pin the man down! 'Out there' has large dimensions in a planetary war. What particular part of it are you concerned with?"

Dodd was silent for a moment. " 'Were,' he corrected, with a touch of grimness. "That job is finished."

"That's where men of your profession are so lucky," said Webber. "You always have something definite to do, with clear-cut beginnings and ends.

Well, what job? Why not tell us and be done with it?"

"You don't know what you may be letting yourselves in for in asking that question," the other replied, slowly. "Of course, I could tell you the whole business in half a minute . . . but in that case I'd have to leave the significance out. And that's all this experience had, as I see it: significance. There's no story; at least, none of the kind to make you say: 'Go on! What happened next?' No one killed, or torpedoed and cast adrift on a raft. And what *was* killed would not be considered worth a two-inch obituary in any newspaper. Whether you'd be interested or not . . ."

"We're willing to chance that," said Marsh.

"Yes, fire away," said Webber. "If you bore us we'll stand on no ceremony in letting you know about it."

"Don't scare me off before I start," said Dodd, with a faint smile. "I'm no raconteur. I'll be obliged to fumble and grope my way along. I tell you, I learned something on this assignment. It opened my eyes to . . . to what the whole world may be coming to if we go on as we're going now. And how are we to go otherwise? I see no possibility of turning back or changing direction. But . . . well, after the war I'd like to see parts of the planet walled off, so to speak: out of bounds to engineers and all their allied tribes.

Above all, out of bounds to machines. And I don't see that coming," he added, soberly. "The Atlantic Charter had nothing to say of that kind of freedom unless it was implied in freedom of worship. Leave worship aside, if you like. Call it freedom to enjoy life on the human scale, on a planet not wholly wrecked and desolated by machines. Queer talk, isn't it, to be coming from the lips of an engineer? But, as I say, I've had my eyes opened. I'm not the fellow who went out there just a year ago this month. I was away six weeks. The job I was sent out to do required scarcely half the time."

II

I'M GOING ALL THE WAY back to boyhood for the start ... not of the story, such as it is; for *my* start, our start, the three of us sitting here. Phil, you were speaking at dinner of the so-called lost generation, the post-World-War-I generation that left its teens, or was about to leave them, just as the century was leaving its own. They made quite a noise about being lost, those youngsters; it became a kind of profession for them. But it strikes me that men of our vintage — women too for that matter — now in their late or middle fifties, have a better claim to the doubtful distinction of being lost. We were in the unhappy position of passing boyhood in one era and manhood in another, with a gulf of change between the two such as, I believe, has never before separated the youth and manhood of individuals in all the history of the human race. Who could have guessed, say around eighteen ninety-five, how soon and how swiftly the change was to come? We had another ten years to know the kind of life our fathers and grandfathers had known. Call it fifteen years. Centuries are never clear-cut divisions between eras. The nineteenth, as I see it, ended at the close of the first decade of the twentieth. Our roots were firmly embedded in the soil of the nineteenth.

I don't mean to lament here the passing of "the good old days." As a matter of fact, there never was a young man more content than myself to see them pass. Miracles in the worlds of physics, chemistry, engineering, mechanical achievement of every sort, were happening all around us. We were, as you know, in a state of perpetual awe, wonder, delight, and expectation. It was at this time, nineteen twelve, that I graduated from the engineering school at Massachusetts Tech. I'd passed my boyhood on a farm in Michigan. Detroit wasn't so far away, and it was natural that I should want to return to that growing expanding heaven for engineers, draughtsmen, and machines with internal-combustion engines. And so I did, but the boy of the eighteen-nineties, of the horse-and-buggy age, came too. He hadn't much to say, and he had less and less to say as time went on; but he was still there.

Enough about the past. All I need to add is that, with the exception of the year the three of us spent in France during the last war, Detroit has been my home.

It was in March last year that I left for San Francisco and points southwest in the Pacific. No need to remind you of what was happening at that time.

Hong Kong had fallen, Manila had fallen, Singapore had fallen. MacArthur was still holding out on Bataan Peninsula but the end of that resistance against hopeless odds was in sight. The position of the stouthearted Dutch in the East Indies had been equally hopeless; they could receive no effective aid from us, after Pearl Harbor. It then seemed by no means impossible that the sea route from Canada and the U.S.A. to Australia via Honolulu, Samoa, and Fiji would be lost as well, or, if not lost, rendered so dangerous as to be all but useless until such time as the U.S.A. could build up strength to hold and protect it. An auxiliary route across the Pacific had to be planned and prepared for. A glance at a large-scale chart will show you how that improvised lifeline would have to run, and by what islands and archipelagoes ships, planes, troops, and supplies would have to be routed should the other more direct sea lane be lost. There were vast water gaps that few planes could cross, under their own power, but this problem was to be met in ways I forbear to mention.

I was one of many, I suppose, sent out on this work of hasty improvisation. Actually, there was not a day, not an hour to be lost. I had been a captain in the Eighth Engineers, National Guard, for some years. First thing I knew I was kicked upstairs to a colonelcy and sent on my way at six hours' notice. This advance in rank was merely a matter of expediency, to give me standing with the authorities in the place to which I was being sent; but I was told to fulfill my mission in civilian clothes so as not to attract undue attention to the military aspect of it.

There was nothing political in the assignment; that part of the business had been taken care of in advance. My job was an engineering problem of a quite simple kind. A certain island, a coral island well south of the Equator, was to be transformed into a naval and military base. Upon arriving at this place I was to have a clear two weeks to make my survey and perfect plans against the arrival of the freighter which was to follow loaded with men and equipment to begin work. The freighter was already lying at a pier in Oakland, ready for cargo, on the day I took off by sea plane from the Treasure Island airport.

There was something faintly comical about our hasty departure from San Francisco. Ominous, too: one felt in an almost physical sense the pressure of disastrous events. The plane for the special mission had been commandeered from the Pan American Line; apparently, there were no Army or Navy planes available at that time. There were eighteen passengers. I could detect in the manner of most of them something of the surprise and incredulity that I myself felt at being sent airpost-haste to hitherto unheard-of or undreamed-of destinations. Nearly all of us were last-minute arrivals and the plane had to be held over twenty minutes for the latest comer, a leather-necked Middle Westerner from St. Louis who came by taxi from the San Mateo airport. He had the seat across the aisle from me, and just as we were taking off he leaned over to say: "Guess I was the last of us visiting firemen to come, wasn't I? Damned if they would even give me time to go home for my toilet kit! I'll have to buy a new one in Honolulu."

I was mighty favorably impressed by my fellow passengers. No confidences as to our particular jobs or destinations were exchanged, but there was a tacit taking it for granted that we were all going out on the same general kind of emergency war work. "Visiting firemen" about hit off the situation, I thought. We were being sent out into the widespread conflagration flaming up at scattered points all over the Pacific; not, to be sure, to help extinguish fires already raging, but, if possible, to prevent them from spreading. I had the feeling that these fellows would prove equal to whatever tasks were assigned to them. They appeared to be men used to meeting emergencies, the kind that can be depended upon to make quick decisions and get quick results. I hoped that I was half as competent as all of them looked. However, I wasn't worrying much. I knew what was expected of me and that I was well equipped to handle the job. Only one thing gave me concern: ordered off on such short notice there had been no time to learn anything of the outfit that was to follow by ship. I had been assured, though, that all these matters were in competent hands and that the freighter would carry equipment for whatever kind of engineering problem we might have to cope with.

I didn't know why I had been selected for this job. I had done little engineering work outside the U.S.A. and Canada and had never set foot in the tropics. I decided that there was a kind of providence in the event. All my life I had nursed a secret longing to visit the islands of the South Seas. I'd never confessed this to any of my fellow Detroiters. Maybe I was a bit ashamed of it as too romantic a dream for an engineer to cherish. But the dream was always there, under the surface of consciousness.

Strangely enough, at this time I was not at all concerned about the island itself and what was to happen to it. I didn't even try to picture it except in a vague way and never so much as wondered whether it would be inhabited or not. I must have assumed that it was uninhabited, a sort of Wake Island, or Midway, as these had been before the coming of the Pan American Line. Coral islands had played no part in my life. All that I knew about this one was that it had an excellent passage through the reef, wide enough and deep enough to accommodate any ship in the U.S. Navy. I also knew that the lagoon was so many miles long by so many wide, with various islets scattered along the encircling reef. In the mind's eye I saw the place merely as so much reef, land, and water, to be converted for the first time in history to a practical use. I call this curious because of those romantic dreams of islands. I suppose it was the boy of the eighteen-nineties who had indulged in them. The engineer on assignment completely forgot them.

This was my first oversea plane journey. I gained for the first time, so vividly, a sense of the rotundity of the earth: the ocular conception as opposed to the imaginative one, and I began to feel how small the planet really is. I've heard men who have done vastly more traveling by air than I have say that flight only increases one's sense of the vastness of the globe. I don't find it so; least of all did I find it so in this seventy-two-hour journey during which, with various stops en route, I was carried from San Francisco to what is, veritably, one of the ends of the earth. No, I had a growing, sobering realization of limitations. Little more than a century ago the seas were walls months high, even years high. Now they are intervals between lunch and dinner, or breakfast and dinner, shrinking visibly as one looks down upon them like the spaces between the numerals upon the dial of a watch as the minute hand moves from one to the next.

Honolulu was our first stop. There we deposited four of our passengers, all those in uniform, and took on three more. We stopped only long enough to change planes and plane crew; then we were away again. Both arriving and departing we had a clear view of Pearl Harbor. It was an appalling sight. I wondered what had become of those watchdogs, Kimmel and Short. In fact, I'm still wondering, together with some one hundred-odd millions of other Americans. But it's just as well, perhaps, that no scapegoats have been chosen to bear the guilt of what happened at Pearl Harbor. If one is to be selected let it be Uncle Sam himself. All of us Americans, from the greatest to the least, are responsible for that disaster.

I soon lost my sense of direction except in a general way. During the next twenty-four hours it seemed to me that we had zigzagged all over the eastern Pacific, on both sides of the Equator. Our cargo of visiting firemen thinned out: we dropped one here, two there, another somewhere else. I remember vividly the desolate island where the last of my fellow passengers was left. It was nothing more than a sickle-shaped sandbank about half a mile from end to end, protected by fringing reefs, with clumps of starved scrub making shadows black as ink in the midday sun. The fellow from St. Louis was the one to be left there. As we circled over the place in preparation for a landing, with the shadow of the plane circling beneath like the ghost of some prehistoric flying monster, my companion said: "I might have spared myself the trouble of buying that toilet kit." I thought so, too. Water would be far too precious to be used for shaving and brushing his teeth. However, he was furnished with two twenty-five-gallon drums of it from the plane, as well as with a small tent and some cases of food. He was to be picked up again in a week's time. A lonely figure he looked as we took off, standing by his little heap of stores in the blob of shadow made by his broad-brimmed hat. He was the right sort, that fellow. He didn't even bother to turn and wave to us but set out at once to look over the place. A moment later we were miles away.

Six hours after leaving the sandbank we reached my destination. I was not, in fact, set down at the actual destination but at an island some four hundred miles from it. I was to go on from there by sea.

I'll not identify the island. All that need be said here is that it did not seem to belong to our exploited, blasted, war-wrecked planet. If you've done any high-seas flying you will remember how rapidly an island, or group of islands, takes on form and distinctness as you approach at a speed of two hundred and fifty miles per hour. At one moment it is a faint bluish blur against the empty sea, scarcely to be distinguished from the sea itself. The next moment, there it is beneath you, outlined in the most exquisite detail: mountains, deep shadow-filled gorges, reef-enclosed lagoons with every shoal in them a splotch of vivid color. You've not had time to prepare yourself for the incredible sight. A wafer-like film of cloud hung over the very center of this island with the peaks of the two highest mountains thrust through into the clear air above. They gave the impression of floating detached, in a sea of golden light, above the greater island beneath. We passed directly above them, and I had a picture of lonely beauty, of unsullied primitive wildness, that I shall treasure in memory to the end of my days.

The sun was near to setting as we lost height in a long descent out to sea; then we banked to come in over the little port town. We circled it twice and turned once more to skim over the barrier reef that looked so close to the land from high above, so far distant at this near view. The pilot set the plane down as gently as a wild duck settles on a Wisconsin lake; then we taxied to a mooring buoy half a mile from shore to wait for the port doctor.

You know the sudden change in point of view at

the end of a journey by air. As the land rushes up to meet and enclose you, the impersonal detached feeling of being a mere spectator of earth, outside the lives and interests of your fellow men, is immediately lost. You are again caught and enmeshed with them, one atom amongst the millions that people the earth. Five minutes earlier the island had looked scarcely large enough to stretch one's legs over in an after-dinner stroll. Now I was gazing up at mountains that looked remote and immensely high, rising as they did so abruptly from sea level. They hemmed in the little town with its strip of foreshore, fronting the lagoon. I had a happy sense of strangeness, of "otherness," so to speak, due to the fact that I had traveled in so brief a time from a great continental city to a crumb of land lost in the midmost Pacific; to a little world as different as possible from anything I had ever known before. Twenty or thirty schooners, cutters, and other small craft were moored along the sea wall. It was a charming place, what I could see of it from offshore, with the fronts of scattered shops, public buildings, warehouses and dwellings, all in various pale colors, taking the westering light. I caught glimpses of old-fashioned horse-drawn vehicles: carts, buggies, surreys, and the like, moving slowly along beneath the trees. It gave me the feeling of having flown straight back to boyhood. The sound of a clear-toned bell, striking the hour from a church tower hidden amongst the trees, was as golden as the air it traveled through.

One of the co-pilots came back to open the door in readiness for the doctor, and we stood together, looking toward the beach.

"Guess we're making quite a stir here, Mr. Dodd," he said. "Look at the crowd along the waterfront!"

I asked if he had called here before.

"Never," he said, "and I don't know any other pilot that has. This place is away off any transpacific air lane. Shouldn't wonder if we're making history. This is probably the first plane that's ever landed here."

"Did they know we were coming?" I asked.

"Yes, but not what day; not even what week. We wirelessed them a couple of hours ago; our orders were not to wireless until we were two hours off. But they've got aviation gas here for us. That was arranged for well in advance."

I gathered from this information that the preparations made from Washington were not as hasty as I had thought, at first.

"Are you spending the night here?" I asked the pilot.

He shook his head. "You're the lucky one. What a pretty little place! I suppose this is the way Honolulu looked in the old days. . . . No, we've got to go on as soon as we fill up and give the engines a quick once-over."

"Where to?" I asked.

"I said, 'on,'" he replied, with a grin.

I was sorry to be leaving them. I'd gotten well acquainted with the plane crew that had taken over at Honolulu; both plane and crew were still of the Pan American service. There were two pilots, of course, a navigating officer, and one engineer. We even had one of those engaging little stewardesses, as pretty as she was competent. All of them were mere kids in comparison with myself, but they had a maturity that impressed me, owing, I suppose, to the nature of their work. But it seemed to me that they had lost the faculty for wonder. This far-reaching special mission could have been no routine flight for them, but they took it all as a matter of course, as young people take everything in these days. However, I may be wrong about this. They carried a burden of responsibility that was off my shoulders. They lacked the free mind I had to wonder and enjoy. Now they were away again for Lord knows where, but the pilot said they would reach the place a little after daylight next morning. They were to have a real "spell" there.

It did look as though all the population of the island had gathered at the waterfront. About ten minutes later a skiff put off to us from the landing steps. The man at the oars was a husky native; the other two were the doctor and an aide to the governor of the place. The medical examination was a half-minute formality; then I said good-bye to the plane crew and got into the skiff to go ashore. The governor's aide informed me that the governor had gone to the far side of the island and there'd not been time, after receiving the wireless from the plane, to get word to him. He was expected to return early next morning.

The crowd by the landing steps opened up to let us through. They were natives, mostly, with a sprinkling of whites and Chinese. They thought I was somebody all right, the only passenger in a huge plane like that. I shouldn't wonder if they considered me a special envoy of President Roosevelt himself. I could see, from the expressions of astonishment on all their faces, that the arrival of the plane was an extraordinary event here. The face of the governor's aide fairly shone with reflected glory as he conducted me along the street to a near-by hotel. We chatted there for a moment or two; then he took his leave, saying he would call for me a quarter of an hour before the time set for the meeting with the governor next morning. It would probably be at ten o'clock.

The hotel was just what I thought it should be for that far-off island. It didn't belong to the twentieth century. I got a great kick out of the place and the landlord who ran it. There were wide verandas upstairs and down running the length of the building with spacious high-ceilinged rooms opening upon them. I was the only guest and the first one, the landlord said, in more than a year. The war had stopped all tourist traffic long since. I had my choice of rooms and selected one opening on the front veranda having a glorious view across the lagoon to the westward. The landlord brought up his battered old hotel register, dating from 1902, for me to sign, and in the next ten minutes he gave me a large slice of his family history, going back nearly a century to the time when his great-grandfather, a Scotchman, had settled in the islands. I could see that there had been a bounteous infiltration of Polynesian blood since those days, but the landlord seemed as proud of his Scotch ancestry as though he had been born at Inverness.

My room contained a lumpy double bed, a marble-topped washstand with a bowl and pitcher on it, a built-in wardrobe, an old-fashioned bureau, two chairs upholstered in faded green plush, and a strip of matting on the bare floor. Over the bed hung a large oil painting of a stag against a background of wild heathy mountains. I got a whiff of genuine emotion from that painting, and the inscription on a brass plaque beneath it stirred me even more: —

> The stag at eve had drunk his fill
> Where danced the moon on Monan's rill,
> And deep his midnight lair had made
> In lone Glenartney's hazel shade.

There was another vivid reminder of boyhood days. "The Lady of the Lake" had been my first unforgettable introduction into the world of poetry.

The hotel was as clean as it was bare, but floors, walls, and ceilings had been so riddled by termites that little more than the paint was holding it together. As I walked gingerly down the back stairway to the shower bath I more than half expected the building to collapse gently in a heap of wood dust with me in the middle of the heap.

Except for morning coffee no meals were served in the hotel, so I went along to a restaurant for my dinner. The street was quite deserted now, everyone having gone to the wharf where the plane was refueling. The restaurant was a frame building built on piles over the lagoon. It was somewhat past the dinner hour but there were still half a dozen people at their meal. All of them, it seemed to me, had an unmistakable island stamp upon them. The peace and quiet of that lonely place seemed to be written upon their faces and their movements were those of people who have never known what it is to hurry.

I had a table by a window giving a wide view of the harbor. I've often read, and heard, that night comes swiftly in the tropics, but it was not so here. The sun had set a good half hour before but the afterglow was still glorious. When I thought it was dying away, came a spectacular resurgence of light as though the sun had changed its mind about setting for good. Wisps of ribbed cloud high in the west and the sky between them took on again the most gorgeous coloring. I had never before seen such an amazing renewal of the afterglow. It was due, I suppose, to some peculiar atmospheric condition.

Just as I was finishing my soup came the roar of the motors of the plane: first one, then another, then all four together, ripping the silence of that peaceful little place into a thousand shreds. I felt suddenly awestruck, and the thunder of such mighty engines is in all truth an awe-inspiring sound wherever heard. Even when accustomed to it one can scarcely grasp the ominous fact that man has been able to harness such power.

The pilots had wasted no time in refueling so that they could take off while there was still light enough to see by. The huge plane moved slowly away from the wharf and when just opposite the restaurant turned westward; then they gave her full motor. I thought the restaurant would be blown right off its foundations. Hats, tablecloths, napkins, and menu cards flew every which way in the powerful backwash from the propellers, and they had scarcely settled to the floor when we saw the plane far in the distance, a black silhouette as it rose swiftly across a band of ashy crimson light. Then it was gone.

There was an event in the history of that crumb of land in the backwaters of the Pacific: an event of evil omen, but I did not think of that at the time. From the abashed glances thrown in my direction by the other diners, you might have thought that I was the man who had dreamed, invented, perfected, and superperfected that great bird; and I was human enough and American enough to enjoy the moment. However, I went on with my dinner with commendable modesty for such a great man. I had a dish of excellent freshwater shrimps with French dressing, and roast pork with baked bananas and breadfruit to follow. I didn't know what the latter was until the waiter enlightened me, and at the first taste I wasn't sure whether I liked it or not; but doubt vanished with every additional mouthful. It went very well indeed with the good pork gravy. Then I had my first heart-of-palm salad with a mango for dessert. Of all the tropical fruits I've eaten, give me a grafted mango for preference. I certainly enjoyed that first one. I had a double portion sliced from either side of the flat oblong seed, and I ate both down to the rind.

By the time I'd finished dinner the place was empty except for one man seated at the table next to mine. I'd noticed him looking me over pretty closely during the meal and when the others had gone we fell into conversation.

"No need to ask if you came by the airship," he said. "Couldn't have been anyone else."

"Airship" gave me an added sense of remoteness from the world I'd left three days earlier. I was reminded of a time that seemed to belong to a previous existence, when Santos-Dumont was making such a stir in the world by his flights in the first crude dirigible, and "airship" began to have some currency in common speech.

"Are strangers here as scarce as that?" I asked.

He nodded, without speaking again for some time; then he said: "My name's Boyle. I'll be seeing you at the governor's tomorrow. It's my island you're going to."

I pricked up my ears at that, but expressed only polite interest. You wouldn't have set him down as being the proprietor of anything much, least of all an island. His suit of white drill was clean, but collar and cuffs had been frayed with long use and both coat and trousers had been patched and darned in many places. He looked like a superannuated bookkeeper, and he spoke in a slow, hesitating manner as though he found it hard to collect his thoughts even for a simple statement. I judged him to be in his late seventies; his hair was silvery white with a yellowish tinge, and face and hands had the waxen pallor of a man who has aged badly. He rarely gave me the direct glance but when he did I had the impression of vitality slowly and painfully gathered up to be shot out in the fraction of a second when his eyes met mine. His were as blue and cold as polar ice.

"I'm an American, too," he volunteered, presently. "Been out here forty-five years. Don't know as I'd want to see another forty-five; or even five more. Looks to me as if this was the end of things as I've known them."

"The end? How's that?" I asked.

"That airship . . . What do you think, yourself? No place too far for 'em to go, is there?"

"No; not in these days," I said.

"Won't they be flying all over the Pacific in a few more years?"

"It strikes me as likely," I replied. "Wouldn't you like that? Suppose you want to go to San Francisco: you can have your dinner here in the evening and land at the Oakland airport in time for breakfast next morning."

"Don't know as I'd relish the breakfast much. I'd be thinking of all the tourists and trippers flying this way at the same time, leaving their Sunday newspapers and lunch boxes and paper napkins all over the place. This is the only world we've got. I don't believe in makin' it so small."

"Well," I said, "I'm afraid there's nothing you and I can do about that."

When he spoke again, his voice had more heat in it than I had supposed his dry old carcass contained.

"No, we can't," he said. "That's the hell of it!"

A moment later he gave me a curt nod and went out.

A lamp with an old-fashioned china globe stood lighted on the bureau when I returned to the hotel. I was tired after my long journey but upon examining the lumpy bed with the springs making hillocks of the thin mattress, I decided to sit up for a while. The painting of the Stag at Eve looked even more beautifully romantic by lamplight than it had by daylight. I don't know whether it was an original or a copy, but whoever the artist, he had worked with love and deep feeling. My thoughts went traveling farther and farther away from the present moment; all the way back to boyhood. I saw our sitting room at home, as it was in those days, lighted by the hard-coal burner and just such a china-globed lamp as the one before me; the family seated around the table, my mother darning stockings, my brothers and sisters reading or studying next day's lessons. I saw myself with my father's fine illustrated edition of Scott's Poems on my knees as I read "The Lady of the Lake" for the first time.

Harp of the North! that mouldering long hast hung
On the witch-elm that shades Saint Fillan's spring . . .

Nothing read in all the intervening years has ever stirred me as those lines stirred me in boyhood. Then, in the curious instantaneous way in which one memory calls up another, I saw myself at school with Tilson's Geography open on the desk before me. "Atoll — a Coral Island," the inscription read, and the engraving above showed such an island as it was supposed to be. A perfect circle of reef-connected islets were geometrically spaced around the enclosed lagoon, with clumps of coconut palms growing here and there and sea fowl skimming over the breakers piling high along the reef. I don't believe that I had once recalled that sketch since boyhood days, but here it was again, floating bright and clear on the surface of consciousness. And not only that. A moment later another entrancing landscape came into view, an illustration for the lines of a poem in Appleton's Fourth Reader, I think it was: either that or McGuffey's: —

Great wide, beautiful, wonderful world,
With the wonderful waters round you curled,
And the wonderful grass upon your breast,
World, you are beautifully drest.

You friendly Earth, how far do you go
With your mountains and plains and the rivers that flow;
With cities and gardens and wonderful isles
And people upon you for thousands of miles?

I'm not sure that I've quoted exactly, but the wording isn't far off. I doubt whether the children of these days have that feeling of awe and wonder and delight, when they think of Mother Earth, that was common to us as kids. They know only too well how far the planet goes, or doesn't go, and the precise number of hours and minutes needed to reach any part of it. These memories thronging back so unexpectedly gave me a strange, confused emotion, happy and unhappy at the same moment. I'd been too busy with engineering problems; with life as it was, and is, and, I suppose, as it will continue to be, only more so, in our industrialized world, to think often of life as we knew it in boyhood. It was on this same evening that I became uneasily aware of the thickness of the shell, or crust, I'd grown after thirty years of engineering. It was a crust composed of oil, cement, emery dust, steel filings, rust, carbon-monoxide gas, and all the soot and thick greasy smoke belched from the chimneys of hundreds of smelters and refiners. It had been proof against any vivid memories of the past. Perhaps it was Monan's rill glittering in the moonlight that washed this first channel through it.

III

I WILL PASS BRIEFLY OVER the next morning's conference with the governor. As I've said, all arrangements for taking over the island had been made in advance by our State Department; my talk with the governor concerned only the practical details of the business. He was courteous enough, but I could see that he was far from happy over this intrusion demanded by the harsh necessities of war. However, he was extremely businesslike and had everything down in black and white, even to the smallest details. It was a kind of leasing arrangement for the duration, and I was given full authority to make whatever changes might be necessary for converting the island into a base. When the war ended it was to be returned, and all installations such as wharves, hangars, barracks, machine shops, electric power plants, and the like were to be handed over to the government having sovereignty there. Boyle was at the conference, and I learned that he was, in fact, the sole owner of the island. He stood to profit handsomely by the arrangement. A schooner was ready to take me

LOST ISLAND

to my destination and I was told that I could leave the same evening if I wished to.

Boyle and I came away from the conference together. He was a curious fellow; I couldn't make him out. There were, naturally, all sorts of questions I wanted to ask about the island, but he put me off with the briefest of replies or none at all. I had taken it for granted that he would be coming too, but he soon made it clear that he had no intention of doing so.

"No," he said; "no more traveling for me till they take me to the local boneyard."

The conference had tired him and when we reached the waterfront he suggested that we rest for a bit on a bench there.

Presently he said: "There's one thing I want to speak about." He was silent for so long I thought he'd forgotten what he meant to say, but at last he added: "I've got a nice place out there . . . on my island, I mean. Used to spend two or three months on it every year. There's a man and his daughter looking after it for me now. . . . I hope they won't have to be disturbed?"

I told him I could make no promises about that, in advance.

"No . . . I don't suppose you can," he replied, slowly. "Well . . . that's all. . . . I just wanted you to know about them." At last he looked up at me with the bleakest smile I've ever seen on a human face.

"When I sent 'em out there," he said, "I thought I was doing a good turn for once in my life. . . . Guess I was too late makin' a start."

He left me a moment later without any explanation of what he meant by that statement.

The last leg of the journey was made in a two-masted, ninety-ton schooner used in the copra and pearl-shell trade amongst those islands. The only other passenger was the Resident Agent of the island I was bound for. His Christian name was Viggo and he was always called so, either that or "Papa Viggo." He was a Dane with a round ruddy face and hair so blond it was almost white. His big belly was as sound as the rest of him. "My heart," he called it; then he would smile and give it a resounding thump with his fist. When I knew him better I was convinced that a heart as big and kindly as his could have found room in no other part of his anatomy. I should not be surprised if, in Viggo, heart and stomach had been fused into one organ, digesting food and experience together, and never with the slightest touch of spleen. There are certain men who, you know at first glance, are good all the way through. Viggo was one of these. I never heard him say an unkind word of anyone.

The captain of the schooner was also called only by his first name — Tihoti, which is the native word for "George." Viggo and George — what a pair they made! They were contemporaries in age, around sixty, but George, although he had the point of view of a white man, had a considerable mixture of Polynesian blood in his veins. He had a walrus mustache and bloodshot, protruding blue eyes that glared at you in a manner disconcerting at first until you learned that there was nothing hostile behind the glare. He was one of the most naturally courteous men I've ever met — that is, in his attitude toward strangers; with Viggo, of course, he stood on no ceremony since they had been friends from away back. There was a courtly, Old World charm about him, and while he could remove that manner as easily as taking off his coat, I became convinced that it was no veneer of good breeding but something native; a gift received, probably, through his Polynesian blood.

Before we had been an hour at sea I was on excellent terms with these two old cronies. I soon gathered that they had only a vague notion of the nature of my errand. They knew that some kind of base was to be made on the island, but their idea of it was a storage tank or two to contain fuel oil for ships that might have to pass that way now and again. I decided not to give them the facts until I had to.

The captain had a short-wave radio, but it was an old contraption and static was so bad, he said, twenty-five days out of the month, that he didn't bother to listen in often. However, on this first night he tried to get London and succeeded after a fashion. We heard Big Ben striking the hour and the voice of the announcer saying: "This is London calling in the Overseas Service of the B.B.C." After that scarcely a word was distinguishable for several minutes; then we heard: "Some of our overseas listeners have written to ask whether nightingales still sing in wartime England. We are happy to let the nightingales answer that question for themselves." Following that, we heard the faint song of a bird but the static soon drowned it out. The captain switched off the current in disgust.

"I wonder if that was an imitation?" said Viggo. "Surely, they couldn't have had a nightingale right there by the what-you-may-call-it — microphone?"

"Viggo, you're the dumbest man about radios," said the captain. "Of course they didn't have a nightingale there. The song was what they call transcribed, off a phonograph record."

"Was it?" said Viggo, with a blank look. "Is that how they do it?"

Presently he added: "I expect that's all the nightingales' songs they'll have left by the time the war's over: what they've got on the phonograph records. My, my! What a world it is in Europe for the birds, with all the shells and aeroplanes and bombs!"

"I was reading a while back," said the captain,

LOST ISLAND

"about a big flock of aeroplanes that had been making a daylight raid somewhere in France or Belgium. This was last spring. It told about how they'd flown right through a flock of small birds on the way home. They were going so fast they didn't see the birds till they were right amongst 'em. It said all those planes came home plastered with blood and feathers and the bodies of little birds so flattened out they couldn't tell *what* they were."

"What's happening to all the wild life over in Europe, Mr. Dodd?" Viggo asked. "There must be a lot about it in the papers. And the fish? You'd think the fish must be about wiped out in the Mediterranean and the North Sea, with the depth bombs and mines and torpedoes."

I said that I'd seen no mention in the papers of the tragedies of the birds and fishes, but I didn't confess, which was true, that I'd never myself given the matter a thought. It struck me as strange that I'd had to come all this distance to meet anyone who appeared to be concerned about these matters. I changed the subject by asking them to tell me something about Boyle.

The captain heaved himself out of his deck chair to spit over the rail, as though the mere mention of the name had brought a nauseating taste to his mouth.

"That old skunk!" he said. "He's the biggest crook in the Pacific!"

"Now, Tihoti," said Viggo, with an air of mild protest.

"He is," said the captain, with even more heat. "Viggo knows it as well as I do. Mr. Dodd, that fellow has done more dirt in his lifetime than the devil himself could have thought up."

"What about the Lehmanns?" asked Viggo.

"I knew you'd bring them in. Leave them aside for now. One good deed in forty-five years won't make up for all the misery he's caused."

Viggo was about to make another protest but the captain cut him off.

"Just you be quiet, Viggo," he said. "Mr. Dodd ought to know something about Boyle since it's his island he's going to, and I'm the man to tell him, not you."

"*His* island!" he added, bitterly. "He's got the legal rights to it, that's true enough, but if he had his dues he'd be in jail for life. Thirty years ago the natives weren't protected in their property rights the way they are now. Boyle took advantage of that. He was bound to have that island and he got it the way he's gotten everything else he owns, by dirty underhand tricks. He's smart, no doubt about that. He's nobody's fool except his own, and that's the only thing that gives me a grain of comfort when I think about him. Maybe, now when he's just about ready to tumble into his grave, he's beginning to wonder what good all his skulduggery has done him."

"Boyle told me that he had a man and his daughter living on the island, taking care of his house," I said. "Are they the Lehmanns you spoke of just now?"

"Yes," said the captain. "Viggo, you can tell him about them."

I'll not attempt to repeat the story as I heard it that night on the schooner. The captain would break in now and then and the two of them would argue back and forth about the motives that had prompted Boyle to do what he did. By the time I'd been told all the circumstances I had two strangely contrasted pictures of Boyle to set side by side. This is the gist of the tale: —

In the autumn of 1940, shortly after the fall of France, Boyle had gone to the British consul — of the island we'd just left — with a request that nearly bowled the consul over because of its unexpected nature. He said that he wanted to do something for a family of Jewish refugees — any family; it didn't matter about that so long as it was one right up against it: homeless, friendless, desperate, not knowing which way to turn. He wanted the consul's help in bringing such a family out to the islands from Europe. Boyle guaranteed to stand all expenses and he promised to take full responsibility for their support, for the rest of their lives, if need be.

Knowing Boyle well, the consul was more than suspicious. He wondered what kind of shady scheme that he would stand to profit by Boyle was cooking up now. Certain, at first, that there could be nothing altruistic about it, he told Boyle that such a plan was out of the question, in wartime. Continental Europe was in the hands of the barbarians. Switzerland, Spain, and Portugal were the only countries not yet in their clutches. No, it was an impossible plan. Nothing could be done about it.

But Boyle persisted. He came back again and again with his plea. He offered to place one thousand pounds in advance in the consul's hands, as an evidence of good faith. At last the consul became convinced that the man was sincere; that, for once in his life, he really wanted to perform a generous, unselfish act. He promised to see what might be done. The business was outside his consular functions but that didn't matter. The consul was a humane man. If, through his agency, a refuge might be found for one of the tens of thousands of Jewish families homeless in Europe, he was not the man to stay his hand. Having been assured by the governor that there would be no official objections, he wrote a letter explaining the circumstances to the British consul at Lisbon, Portugal, requesting him, if the plan seemed feasible and transportation could be found for such a family, to wireless the fact, whereupon money to cover all expenses would be immediately wirelessed in return.

Nearly a year passed without any reply to this letter. Then came a radiogram: PASSAGE AVAILABLE VIA PANAMA, JEWISH FAMILY. WIRELESS ONE HUNDRED AND FIFTY POUNDS. FATHER, DAUGHTER. NAME, LEHMANN.

They arrived by a small British freighter New Zealand bound, and Captain George had brought them on to Boyle's island. He was in port with his schooner on the day they arrived from Lisbon. He said that Boyle's manner toward the refugees was consideration itself. He showed great delicacy of feeling, effacing himself as much as possible. It was the consul who acted as intermediary. He told them of Boyle's home on the atoll; of his love for the place and how he was now too old and infirm to look after it himself. He wanted a dependable family to live there. They were to have the full use of this home for as long as they chose to remain, with all expenses paid and a small but comfortable salary in addition. They were also informed that the island was a lonely place, having no contact with the outside world save by the schooner that called there twice yearly. It offered no distractions except what they could devise for themselves.

"Mr. Dodd," said the captain, "I wish you could have seen them the day they landed from the freighter. They couldn't believe what was happening. They were afraid to believe in case they might wake up and find it was nothing but a dream. After the horrors they'd been through . . . well, it was just too much, having such kindness shown them. The consul told me how they sat on his veranda, the daughter holding her father's hand, neither of them able to speak from the fullness of their hearts. He said he had to leave them for a bit and fuss around in his office, to give them both time to pull themselves together.

"He'd received a letter from the consul in Lisbon, telling about the Lehmanns. He let me read it. Mr. Lehmann had been a professor in some university in Vienna at the time the Nazis came there. His only brother had been caught, and all he ever heard of him after that was when a box was sent containing his ashes. Mrs. Lehmann was dead. Mr. Lehmann and his daughter, Ruth — she's a beautiful girl, eighteen or nineteen years old — escaped to Czechoslovakia. Then the Huns took that country, and, somehow, they managed to reach Poland. They went on from there, before war broke out, to France, by sea. They hoped they were safe, in France. Mr. Lehmann, who is a fine violinist, got a job playing in some orchestra. Then the Huns came tearing into France and the Lehmanns escaped from Paris just in time. They had a terrible journey from then on. They had no papers and only two hundred francs in money. They managed to cross the Spanish border at night. That was in September, and they made their way over the mountains on foot. How they got into Portugal the letter didn't say."

"Tell him about the piano," Viggo put in.

The captain was silent for some little time.

"That Boyle!" he exclaimed, wonderingly. "That old crook! Whoever would have thought he had a spark of decency in him? But what he's done for the Lehmanns . . . there's just no explaining it. It's one of those things that goes to show how hard it is to size up any man, even when you've known him as long as I've known Boyle. My belief is that the old villain has softened up, now that he knows he hasn't long to live. He's scared, that's the plain truth. He hopes he can ride into heaven on his one good action."

"Tell him about the piano," Viggo repeated.

"I'm coming to that," said the captain, testily. "Give me time.

"There were some Russians crossed this part of the Pacific a few years back. They were refugees, too. They'd had to leave Russia at the time of the Revolution and had been wandering from one place to another ever since. They came out here from Shanghai and were trying to get to South America. But they were just about busted, and the only thing they had left that could be turned into money was a fine piano. . . . What's it called, Viggo?"

"A Bechstein."

"That's it. They'd held onto it as long as they could and it just about broke their hearts to part with it. Boyle bought it on spec. Here's another thing I haven't told you about that fellow: he has a real love for music. He can't play a note, himself, but he has the finest phonograph and the biggest collection of records, I'd say, in the whole Pacific. None of your jazz and cheap stuff: classical pieces, Beethoven, Brahms and Mozart, and all that. He's never had any friends; no one ever goes to see him except on business, and that's how he spends his evenings, playing his phonograph.

"On the evening of the day the Lehmanns came they went with the consul to Boyle's house, and when Miss Lehmann saw the piano she was drawn to it, the consul said, like a starving person at the sight of food. He said he'd never forget that evening, and I guess Boyle hasn't forgotten it either. Mr. Lehmann had a violin, the only thing he'd carried with him all the time they were running from the Huns. That was sent for and father and daughter played the evening through. They couldn't have found a better way of thanking Boyle for what he had done for them. They could say in music what it was hopeless trying to say in words. The consul said that Boyle was like another person, and when they came on to the island by my schooner, he sent the piano with them. I guess it was the one thing needed to make their happiness just about perfect."

"And they like the island? They're really happy there?" I asked.

The captain pondered this question for a moment.

"I don't know that I should have called it happiness," he said. "I'm afraid they've suffered too much ever to know real happiness again. But they think the island is heaven on earth. What's your opinion, Viggo?"

"I'll tell you," said Viggo. "Whenever I see them, and that's nearly every day, I have a warm feeling in my heart for old man Boyle. Whatever he's done before is wiped off the slate, so far as I'm concerned."

"I'm not that much of a Christian," said the captain, grimly. "But I'll give him his due for what he's done for the Lehmanns."

During the course of the voyage I learned of one other white resident of the island. The captain was carrying out half a dozen young fruit trees in tubs, and he and Viggo watered and cared for them as though they were the most precious trees on earth. They told me they were for Father Vincent. Both men spoke of him with a warmth that showed their affection for the old priest who was spiritual adviser to the inhabitants of this and three other atolls within a radius of two hundred miles.

"You'll like Father Vincent," said Viggo. "I'm not a Catholic and the father has never tried to make me one; but the natives are — my wife too. We think the world and all of Father Vincent. He's a Christian first and a Catholic afterward. That's the way it should be, as I see it."

"And he's none of your Scribes and Pharisees kind," said the captain. "Viggo, you remember the time I brought out the young mango and breadfruit trees? I got in with my schooner on a Saturday evening," he added, turning to me. "There'd been a long spell of dry weather, but next morning the rain was pouring down and it kept pouring all day. Father Vincent wouldn't miss a chance like that. He rang the bell for Mass, as usual, but he'd sent word around that no one was to wear Sunday clothes. Instead of going to church he went with the whole congregation to his garden to set out the young trees while the weather favored. He said there was more than one way of worshiping the Lord."

"He's got what they call the planting hand," said Viggo. "His garden is a real wonder, Mr. Dodd. It's not for his private use. Everybody shares in it, the children most of all. There ain't another like it on any of the coral islands. You know, none of the tropical fruits such as bananas, mangoes, breadfruit, papaias, and the like, grow on the atolls. They've got to have rich volcanic soil from the High Islands, so Father Vincent has Tihoti bring him some every time the schooner calls here."

"I've got fifteen tons aboard this trip," the captain added. "I wouldn't be able to guess how much I've brought in all, in the last thirty years. It will be thirty years next June that the father started making the garden. What he's done in that time . . . but you'll have a chance to see it for yourself."

The interests of these two old friends were refreshingly wide from mine and new to me. They talked of islands whose names I had never so much as heard of, scattered over a thousand-mile area in that part of the Pacific, so far removed from steamship routes that the lives of their inhabitants had changed very little from what they had been in heathen times. The captain was born an islander — though his father, a prosperous trader, had sent him to school in England — and Viggo had lived for so long in that lonely sea that no more than George could he conceive of any great change taking place there even in the midst of a planetary war. As for myself, under the influence of their companionship, and lapped round as we were by the peace of mid-ocean, I could almost doubt the reality of what was happening elsewhere in the world. But at times, as I watched the foam patterns moving slowly aft along the sides of the vessel, I would see there the face of that paper hanger, that madman Schickelgruber, or Hitler as he calls himself, who had boasted that Germany would either conquer the world or pull it down in ruin. And I thought with a bitterness common to all of us in these days of the so-called statesmen who, until it was too late, remained so blandly indifferent to all the repeated warnings and danger signals.

Then perhaps Viggo would, to my great relief, break into the current of these musings by speaking of his turtle islet and how eager he was to be at home before the last of the pits of eggs laid by the great sea turtle should hatch. "I hope we get there in time, Mr. Dodd," he would say. "There's a sight worth seeing: when the baby turtles come out."

IV

We sighted the island at dawn on the fourth day, a slender thread of black against the increasing light, and an hour later we were close in with it. The sea was calmer than I had supposed the ocean could ever be, with a few scattered clouds mirrored in it almost to perfection. To a man inland born and bred as I was, there is something almost incredible in the first sight of a coral island, particularly such a one as this, far out on the Pacific, thousands of miles from the nearest continent. It gives you a deep emotion. It's as though you had sailed right off the planet. I forgot Detroit, the U.S.A., the war, and the errand that brought me here. I had . . . how shall I put it? . . . a feeling of peace, of deep content. When you see such an island you know for the first time the meaning of the word "loneliness." And if you've lived the kind of life I've lived, you realize of a sudden how long, without guessing it, you've needed to have that meaning brought home to you. It's hard to put into words the sense of a reawakening, of reassurance granted. Believe it or not, for the next hour not one thought of the barbarians, whether German or Jap, crossed my mind.

In order to give me a preliminary view the captain headed the schooner for the northwest extremity of the atoll and we coasted along the leeward side for ten or a dozen miles, just off the reef. There were long stretches of reef awash where I could look across into the lagoon and beyond to the islets on the far side, blurs of pale blue against the horizon. Viggo pointed out one of these to me, his beloved turtle islet, at that distance no more than a faint irregularity against the skyline. The ones on the near side, a dozen or more, were gems of islets, with a few coconut palms and pandanus trees casting long shadows over the coral sand. The sea birds, among them snow-white terns, fluttering over the trees or skimming along the hollows made by the combers rising to break on the reef, gave the one touch of life and movement needed to make loneliness more lonely still.

At length we approached the islet where the village stood. It was a little more than a mile in length, from five to six hundred yards broad, and beautifully green from end to end. No sign of human habitation could be seen from the ocean side. As I have said, the passage through the reef was a wide deep channel, but inside the lagoon we had to thread our way through a number of coral shoals rising to within a fathom or so of the surface. I remember thinking: "Those coral heads will have to be blasted out the first thing we do." I resented being reminded so soon of my errand here. The moment of pure content had vanished, but a moment that has lasted for all of an hour is so much clear gain. I remember reading somewhere a statement — by some crabbed old misanthrope, evidently — to the effect that the man would be lucky who could look back in old age over his life and tally up as much as an hour of unflawed peace of mind enjoyed in the course of seventy years. I had that much in one whack. It's a pity that I had to notice those coral heads or it might have lasted longer.

We moored at a coral-slab pier extending twenty yards across the shallows. At the end of it the lagoon floor fell away steeply to a good fifteen fathoms, more than ample depth for the coming freighter. The uneasy anxious feeling deepened as I thought of the freighter loaded and ready to sail at that same moment, perhaps; or it might even then be moving slowly down San Francisco Bay toward the Golden Gate. With an effort I erased that picture from my mind. I was bound to have at least one day as free as possible from thoughts of what was to come.

The entire population had gathered on the pier and the beach; that is, all the natives. I didn't see the Lehmanns amongst them. But Father Vincent was there, and the first glimpse of him was enough to show why Viggo and the captain had spoken of him with such affection. You felt the influence of his kindly nature from afar. He had snow-white hair and a long white beard, and was dressed in a rusty-looking old soutane and a broad-brimmed pandanus-leaf hat. The smoke curling out from his long-stemmed meerschaum pipe seemed the peace of the island made visible and tangible. There he stood in the midst of his flock, and he looked more native to the place than the natives themselves. Viggo's two grown sons were there to greet him, strapping fellows in their early twenties. Viggo's wife was a Polynesian, born on this island. The boys showed far more of their mother's than of their father's blood, but one of them had Viggo's clear blue eyes.

It was a pleasure to look over that crowd. There was not a sickly looking person amongst them; even the old people, the grandfathers and grandmothers, looked as though they might go on living for another fifty years. They showed a vigor that spoke well for their simple, natural way of life, and both old and young had beautiful teeth, as white as the meat of a coconut. I made a hasty count and estimated the population as numbering between seventy-five and one hundred. Viggo made them a little speech in the native tongue, explaining me, evidently, for as soon as he had finished all the grownups came along to shake hands with smiles and grins of the most evident good will. Father Vincent came too and gave me a cordial welcome, but I could see that what chiefly interested him at the moment were the fruit trees the captain had brought him. He was delighted to find them in such flourishing condition, and immediately commandeered the services of some of the boys to carry them to his garden.

When the greetings were over I went with Viggo to his house with most of the children tagging along at our heels. The houses were scattered along the lagoon beach, and the beach itself, of hard-packed coral sand, was the village street. It was shaded with gnarled old trees that looked as though they had been growing there always. Outrigger canoes, from small two-men craft to large sailing canoes that would accommodate a dozen or more, were drawn up in the shade, and fishing nets hung from the branches of the trees. The little settlement was scrupulously clean; it looked as though it were swept from end to end every morning. The dwellings were all of palm-frond thatch and behind each one was the *faré-himaa*, as they call them — open-sided huts with thatched roofs over the earth ovens where the household cooking is done.

Viggo's house stood midway in the village. His was the only frame building in the settlement. There were wide verandas both front and back and the whole was roofed with corrugated iron. Here I met Mrs. Viggo and their three daughters, girls in their teens, all of them chips off the old block in health and sturdiness. Mrs. Viggo was almost as large as her husband but a lively active body for all that. She took my hand in both of hers and addressed me volubly in the native tongue, breaking off to laugh heartily when her husband reminded her that I could not understand a word she was saying. A moment later she bustled off to the cookhouse to see about the preparations for the morning meal.

It was eleven o'clock when we drew up at table, Viggo, the captain, and I, and what a meal it was! In quantity, at least, it reminded me of the farm dinners of the Middle West at harvest time, and here as there the womenfolk waited on table, having their meal when the men had finished. We had four kinds of shellfish, including lobster, half a dozen kinds of baked and broiled fish, roast suckling pig with Low Island taro, curried chicken and rice, and I don't know what all else, ending up with a kind of sweet pudding — *poi* they call it — with a sauce of coconut cream. I'm a pretty good trencherman, but I was nowhere with Viggo and the captain. It was a memorable sight to watch them storing away provender as though they expected to fast for the next week.

"Mr. Dodd," said Viggo, "if you like we might go over to see the Lehmanns this evening. I'll let them know you've come."

"You think they wouldn't mind?" I said.

"No, no. They're fine hospitable people. Mr. Lehmann doesn't know English very well, but Ruth does; and her father can speak every language with his violin. We can hear some music if you'd care to?"

"I'd like nothing better," I said.

"Miss Lehmann has a lovely voice," said the captain. "She knows all the fine old songs, in French, English, or German. I could listen all night, the way she sings them."

"Life here must have seemed very strange to them at first," I said.

"Yes, it did," said Viggo, "but they've taken to it in a way that's surprised me. They're city folks born and bred. I thought they'd be very lonely here, but they're not. They're so simple and natural in their ways, I guess they could fit themselves in anywhere. Everybody likes them. Mr. Lehmann's not a strong man. He doesn't come over to the village very often, but Ruth does. It's wonderful the way she's learned the native language in these few months. She's a very bright girl."

Having finished his *poi*, Viggo scraped his plate for the last drop of coconut cream, then pushed back his chair with a groan of content. The captain looked even more apoplectic than usual. He took a cushion from one of the sofas and stretched out on the bare floor of the veranda.

"We always have a siesta after *kaikai*," said Viggo. "Too hot to do anything else in the middle of the day. My wife's got your room ready if you want to have one yourself."

I've never formed the siesta habit, but I could well understand its value to the inhabitants of a coral island. With no breeze blowing, the hours in the middle of the day are, to say the least, enervating, the coral sand reflecting back fiercely the heat of the sun. But the trade wind was now blowing freshly again, ruffling the surface of the lagoon to the deepest blue. To a man like myself, used to the temperatures of July and August in the Middle West, the air seemed gratefully cool. Nevertheless, I went to the room Mrs. Viggo had prepared for me and sat for a while by the open window, thinking of one thing and another. Little I'd dreamed, that day a week ago, what the week was to have in store for me. I was in Chicago on the twentieth floor of a hotel on Michigan Avenue on the day the wire came of my appointment to this job. A greater contrast than that between the landscape I saw from my hotel bedroom and the one framed by the window of Viggo's guest room could scarcely be imagined.

LOST ISLAND

This struck me as a good time for a stroll. I would have the island pretty much to myself, so I went quietly out past Viggo and the captain, stretched out sound asleep on the veranda floor, puffing and blowing like a pair of grampuses. Leaving the beach I came to a broad straight path leading down the center of the islet, and at the end of it I could see Father Vincent's church.

Not a soul was stirring anywhere. I spied sleeping forms on mats by the doorways of the thatched houses or lying in the shade outside. As I was to learn, the siesta habit was a universal one here, but at night the people were up at all hours; often they would have supper at midnight or breakfast at two o'clock in the morning, the light of their fires casting wavering shadows among the stems of the coconut palms. I came upon a group of children, five- and six-year-olds, asleep in the middle of the roadway. They made a pretty picture with the checkered shadows moving to and fro across their faces and their chubby brown arms and legs. They had been playing some kind of hopscotch game common to children the world over, for the hard-packed coral sand where they lay had been marked off into squares. One little fellow had the end of a bark string tied around his wrist as though he had been afraid the wagon attached to the other end might go off without him while he slept. The body of the wagon was the half of a coconut shell beautifully smoothed and polished, mounted on a framework of sticks. Segments, perfectly round, cut from some kind of snail shell, served as wheels. It was no hodgepodge of a child's toy but one most ingeniously put together. I could see that it had been a labor of love and skill and wondered whether so small a child could himself have made it.

None of the children stirred as I walked quietly around them. It's curious how the picture they made lingers in the memory. Perhaps it was because of the setting, so strange and new to my Northern eyes, with nothing anywhere to remind me of the twentieth century. I had the feeling of having strayed by accident into some last lost remnant of the Golden Age that Time had overlooked.

The church I came to a quarter of a mile farther on did little to mar the illusion. Worship must have played an important part in the lives of men during the Golden Age, if ever there has been one, and the temple I saw before me seemed to express the very spirit of worship. I had been told by Viggo and the captain that Father Vincent had himself designed and built it, with the help of his congregation, twenty-five years before, and that, with the exception of the bell and the stained-glass windows, all the materials came from the island itself. It was a coral-lime structure — that is, the walls, three feet thick, were of coral slabs cemented together and smoothed outside and in with a lime of burnt coral, as white as snow. There were five tall Gothic windows on either side and an oriel window at each end. The bell tower was in perfect proportion with the rest of the building; in fact, the only part to offend the eye was the steep-sloped roof of corrugated iron. That was a concession to necessity, for there is, of course, no running water on a coral island. It is a precious commodity, supplied by such roofs as are made to catch the rainfall, and carried to reservoirs built underground. I had seen the community reservoir for the village which collected the rainfall from its own broad roof and that from Viggo's house. By the church was a second one with a capacity, I judged, of around ten thousand gallons.

The door of the church stood open. The cool dim interior enclosed the peculiar kind of silence and peace that a small church can hold as well as the greatest of cathedrals. It was made the more impressive by the slow ticking of a clock which stood in a recess between two of the windows, saying: "Forever . . . and ever . . . and ever . . . and ever," as though it were speaking from an anteroom of Eternity itself. I walked up the center aisle to examine the altar which must have been a labor of years to complete. It was of dark paneled wood and in the center of each panel was a rosette or fleur-de-lis exquisitely carved from pearl shell. The borders were also inlaid with mother-of-pearl, hundreds of small oblong or diamond-shaped pieces to make, with the wood, a tessellated frame for the central ornament of each panel.

I spent half an hour in the church, thinking of the old priest who had built it as a monument to his faith, on an island so far from the ancient home of that faith. And a fitting monument it was, but no more so, I thought, than his garden which showed the other side of his nature and his love for Mother Earth. The path by which I had come led directly to the church door. It was continued from the other end of the church and passed through the center of the garden. His small house stood at the end of a lawn outside the garden, which was a walled enclosure of several acres. The central walk was shaded throughout by a trellis covered from end to end with flowering vines, and smaller paths bordered by shrubs native to the island led to his groves of High Island fruit trees: mangoes, bananas, papaias, breadfruit, limes, and avocados. There was one orange tree that must have been his particular pride, loaded with fruit just coming to ripeness. The trees had been planted in wide trenches from which the coral sand had been removed and mixed with humus and the volcanic soil brought by the schooner. The whole of the garden had been laid out with an eye to beauty as well as use, and in the center was a little summerhouse furnished with a circular bench where one could sit and survey the whole of it.

Being an engineer, I tried to estimate the number of man hours of work that had gone into the making of such a garden where everything had to be done by hand, with pick, hoe, and shovel, wheelbarrow and watering pot; the trees to be planted and the very soil brought little by little from a distance of four hundred miles. I was not able to make even a rough guess, but I had no doubt whatever as to the speed with which all this could be swept away — church, garden, everything; the labor of thirty years wiped out in scarcely more than that number of hours. That was my task and it was coming; it would have to come. And not only that: the whole of the village islet would have to be laid waste as well. This first view was enough to show that it offered no more than bare room for the base I had come to prepare. Land planes as well as amphibians were to be stationed here, and the island was to be a refueling depot for long-range bombers and transport planes that might, in the course of events, have occasion to use it. Hangars, repair shops, barracks, radio station, fuel-storage tanks, and other installations would require every square yard of ground not needed for the landing field.

I walked slowly on to the end of the islet, sick at heart at thought of the task ahead, lamenting the chance that had selected me for this work of vandalism demanded by the necessity of war. I was in a mood to curse our so-called Industrial Civilization and all its works, concerned for nothing but itself, for nothing but greater and yet greater room for its own monstrous growth. For the first time in my life I saw it as a cancerous organism, desolating the earth, defiling the rivers, laying waste the forests, poisoning the air with its foul breath, and all the while reaching farther and farther out to clutch and destroy even such crumbs of land as this.

Bitter words — what? No kind of talk for the engineer who had joined so heartily in singing hosannas in the heaven of Detroit where the angels and archangels were casting down their golden crowns around the glassy seas of molten metals that would be the bigger and better machines of tomorrow. "How lovely are the messengers that bring us the gospel of Mass Production!" — no one had joined in that earth-shaking anthem with more enthusiasm than myself, in times past. But Dodd the true believer became Dodd the Doubter, almost the Apostate, in the course of one afternoon, and it was the full realization of the task immediately ahead that made him one.

A few moments ago, Charlie, you were envying engineers because we have definite jobs to do, with clear-cut beginnings and ends. So we have, commonly, and never before had I seen so clearly, as in this case, the end before ever the beginning was made. But you would not have envied me here. Decidedly not! I wish the pair of you might have stood with me in that unspoiled mid-ocean sanctuary as it was on this same afternoon. Thus far, old Father Neptune had been able to keep it inviolate. He had selected very carefully its handful of human inhabitants. But he neglected to examine the passport of one George Dodd, and this latest comer could see at a glance what a neat little job had been given him this time. But I was not what would be called happy in the prospect. I saw in the mind's eye two appallingly contrasted pictures: Before Treatment — After Treatment, and I much preferred the first.

There is a small bird, common, I'm told, to the atolls, one of the few land birds to be found on them. They are extremely shy and it is hard to catch a glimpse of one as they fly from thicket to thicket; but you hear them at intervals. Their song is a lonely, melancholy cry always the same: "Oh-h-h-h . . . Oh-h-h-h . . . Oh-oh-oh-oh-oh-oh," dying away to silence. I heard one during this walk, and it said all I had to say, all there was to say, about the future of . . .

I came very near being indiscreet. I was about to give you the native name of the island. It's a beautiful-sounding name as the natives pronounce it, and it had for them a peculiar significance connected with the legendary history of the Polynesian race. But it has nothing whatever to do with the non-legendary history of nineteen forty-two, so it may as well be forgotten here.

I had a strange meeting before returning from my walk. At the far end of the islet I came upon a hut in the shade of a huge tree that looked to be coeval with the island itself. An area of wildwood here showed what the whole island had been in ancient times when Nature did the planting as she chose. It was not a thicket exactly, for the soil of those islands is not rich enough to permit any great profusion of vines and shrubs and trees. You see no bitter struggle for plant existence; rather, there seems to be a live-and-let-live policy amongst those hardy varieties that have adapted themselves to such localities. Plant society appears to resemble human society found in places where food is scarce: the inhabitants learn to share it in common for the good of all. This so-called wildwood looked as you would expect some long-deserted formal garden to look: the chance grouping of masses of rich green growing from the white coral sand gave the clear spaces winding amongst them the appearance of garden paths that had once been laid out in a kind of maze.

I saw the prints of bare feet in the vicinity of the hut, but no other sign of an occupant except a mat spread over the sand in one corner, with a curiously carved wooden headrest at the end of it. A small wooden chest stood against a wall. That was all the furniture the place contained.

I crossed the end of the islet from the ocean beach to the lagoon beach and presently sat down to examine at leisure a plant of a delicate shade of green and as exquisitely formed as a snow crystal. I had seen the same design, carved from a pearl shell, in the central panel of Father Vincent's altar and wondered where he could have gotten the pattern. The plant grew from pure white sand and lay as flat upon it as though it were the green shadow of something invisible above. For all my efforts to distract my thoughts from the task ahead, I found myself picturing one of the huge caterpillar tractors that would soon be crashing its way through this small paradise of an island, crushing by the score the hermit crabs, and the tiny iridescent lizards that were common here, and grinding into the sand vines and shrubs and such little miracles of plant life as the one I had been examining. I have the habit of talking to myself when alone, and on this occasion I exclaimed aloud: "What a pity! What an everlasting shame!"

Glancing up at that moment my heart skipped a beat

upon seeing an old native seated cross-legged beneath a tree not three paces distant. His only garment was a faded waistcloth, and his emaciated brown body blended so perfectly with the mottled sunlight and shadow that I had to look more closely to convince myself he was not an optical illusion. I had the foolish feeling of one caught talking to himself, but the old native gave no sign that he had heard me or was even aware of my presence; he gazed straight before him as though lost in the depths of reverie. His hair was thick and snow-white and his face such a maze of fine lines and wrinkles as to be completely expressionless. Not knowing what to say in that presence I said nothing, but got to my feet and walked quietly away. When at some distance I turned for a backward glance. I could no longer see him and half doubted that there had been anyone to see in the first place.

It was late afternoon when I returned to the village end of the islet. Passing again through Father Vincent's garden I found him there hard at work; he had just finished planting and watering the young trees the captain had brought him. A procession of young fellows was going to and from the schooner carrying copra bags filled with the High Island earth we had brought as well. The father greeted me in the frank cordial manner that banishes at once the feeling of strangeness between strangers.

"Mr. Dodd," he said, "you come just at the right moment, but my old bones would say, *after* the right moment. They've been crying 'Rest!' for the past half hour."

He led the way to a bench beneath one of his trees that spread its branches in a wide-reaching dome, like the canopy of an umbrella.

"You know this tree?" he asked.

I confessed that I did not.

"It's a jam-fruit," he said. "I had that from Professor Harrison Smith, of the island you've just come from. You know him, perhaps?"

"No, Father," I said. "I'm a complete stranger in this part of the world. This is my first visit to the tropical Pacific."

He gave me a scrutinizing glance from beneath his shaggy eyebrows.

"And you . . . you are traveling for pleasure?"

I shook my head and remarked: "I wonder whether there is anyone in the whole wide world traveling for pleasure in these days?"

There was an opening, a chance to confess the truth of my mission here. I knew that I should take it, that nothing was to be gained by putting off the evil moment; but to announce to the old priest thus brutally, at our first meeting, that all he had labored so hard to accomplish here, together with the life of this small island world as it had existed for centuries, was to be swept away, cease to exist . . . I couldn't do it. Although he may have had some curiosity as to the purpose of my coming, I was convinced that he had no slightest suspicion of the truth. Apparently, Viggo had not yet told him the little he himself knew.

Father Vincent spoke sadly of the war for a moment or two, but I felt that it was almost as unreal to him as to the natives themselves. He had never left his island parish since first coming here forty years earlier. He received no newspapers or reviews to keep him in touch with events in the outside world, and there was no radio on the island. The little news received came by way of Captain George at the time of his infrequent visits. Presently the father put thoughts of the war aside and proceeded to tell me of his struggle to save the jam-fruit tree that threw its circle of deep shade over the spot where we were seated. Its growth, he said, had been very sickly in the beginning, but at last it had adapted itself splendidly to this strange environment.

"It has been a great triumph for me," he added, happily. "Now I have three others, young trees, coming on — you see? — over there. I am very grateful to Professor Smith; he is a gardener after my own heart. He has just now sent me a young durian, grown from the seed of a tree that he brought, years ago, all the way from Borneo. You know the durian?"

I shook my head.

"It is the fruit with the awful smell," he added, with a smile, "but Professor Smith tells me that the meat is like jellied nectar, once you get it past your nose. But the tree needs the hot moist climate of deep valleys. If I succeed in growing it here, Professor Smith writes that he means to propose me for the *Mérite Agricole*."

"It strikes me that you fully deserve it for what you have already done, Father," I said.

"My friend, I've had all the reward I deserve or need in making this garden," he said. He pointed with his pipestem toward the orange tree I had observed before. Some of the children stood gazing wistfully at the nearly ripened fruit, hanging so easily within reach. "There is my prize," he added. "I had many failures before I brought that fine fellow into bearing. Look at those young rascals! They can hardly wait for the fruit to ripen."

"They have more self-restraint than I had supposed any boys possessed," I remarked. "Do none of them visit your garden at night?"

"Will you believe it?" he said, his eyes twinkling. "They're more dependable than their fathers and mothers. But the orange tree is their particular property; all the fruit is divided equally among them. They act as guardians while it is ripening."

A dozen or more children were at work in the garden, sweeping the paths with homemade brooms of coconut-frond midribs; even the little fellows were helping, collecting the piles of leaves and twigs and carrying them to a pit used as a compost bed, half filled with rotting leaves, coconut husks, and the like. They worked with a will and I could see that they took as much pride in the garden as the father himself.

Presently I inquired about the old native I had seen at the far end of the islet.

"I don't wonder that you thought you might have seen a ghost," said Father Vincent. "That man — his name is Kamaké — is one of the real old heathen from away back. I shouldn't wonder if he's the last of them. How old would you say he is?"

"I doubt if I could make a good guess," I replied. "He looks to be all of a hundred."

"He's older than that, the natives say, but none of them knows for certain. When I first came here he looked almost as old as he does now, and he lived where he does now. He almost never leaves that far end of the islet."

"He's a heathen, you say? How do you feel about that, Father?"

The priest's eyes twinkled as he replied.

"Mr. Dodd, a few heathen are needed in the world, to set good examples for the Christians to try and live up to."

"Are you friends with him?" I asked.

He shook his head, slowly.

"You've seen Kamaké," he said. "Do you think there could be a possibility of friendship? Two are needed for that. No . . . Kamaké doesn't belong to my world. It is not too much to say that he doesn't belong to the Polynesian world of these days."

He went on to say that, some years before, a celebrated Polynesian philologist had visited the island. This man, he said, knew more about the various dialects of the Maori speech than any man living, natives included. From the moment he saw Kamaké he had eyes and ears for no one else.

"And at that time," said Father Vincent, "he learned what no one has ever learned before about the ancient religion of these people. Kamaké told him that he had been advised in a dream by the spirit of his grandfather to reveal the sacred teachings lest they should be lost forever. The record, taken down word for word, as it was recited to him by Kamaké, is truly extraordinary. It was later printed in a small book, the old native text in one column with the English translation opposite. I can vouch for the excellence of the translation. Viggo has a copy. Ask him to let you see it."

The father smiled as he added: "You will understand, my friend, that a priest of the Christian Church might have some explaining to do if such a book were to be found in his own library; but I have read it with the deepest interest. It concerns the old esoteric religion of the Polynesians, the worship of Kiho, their supreme God. That religion was so sacred that the name of Kiho was never mentioned in the presence of the common people. The rites connected with the worship of Kiho were not known to them, either. The sacred songs and chants were known only to the old heathen priests who handed them down by word of mouth from generation to generation. Kamaké is one of the last of those old sages, perhaps the very last, and I knew nothing about it, all those years! In fact, until this account of it was printed, no missionary, Catholic or Protestant, has known anything of the worship of Kiho, except in the vaguest way."

All this was so far outside my customary orbit of interests that I gave the recital no more than polite attention. Father Vincent then took me for a tour of his garden, pointing out fruit trees and ornamental trees, flowering vines and shrubs, that he had acclimated here, giving me, with the delight of a boy, the history of each one. And all the time I was thinking: "How am I to tell him? How?"

I found Viggo sitting on his veranda, his bare feet on the railing, with the air of a man wholly at peace with the world.

"We're in time, Mr. Dodd," he said, in a relieved

voice. "They haven't hatched yet. One of the men went over there yesterday. He's just come back."

I was puzzled for a moment as to what he referred to; then I remembered his precious turtles that he had spoken of so often during the voyage.

"They'll be coming out any day now," he added. "I was thinking I'd go over there tomorrow. If you'd like to come we could make the tour of the lagoon and visit all the *motu* along the far reef."

"Good!" I said. "That will suit me fine."

Before I go on, I'd better explain *motu*. It's the native word for "islet"; any fragment of land, large or small, on the reef or in the lagoon is called a *motu*. The word came to have a particular significance for me. It seems to express better than "islet" the nature of such crumbs of land: their peace and beauty and sunlit tranquillity. There's a feel of mid-ocean in the word.

"I've been sitting here just looking at things," said Viggo. "My, my! How good it feels to be home again!"

"You've learned, then, to call it home?" I asked.

"Yes, long since. Next July I'll have been twenty-five years in this one place, and I've never gone back to Denmark in all that time. I used to plan to go, and once I did make a start. That was in nineteen twenty-eight. I expected to be away the best part of a year and was all stirred up thinking of the happy time I'd have seeing Copenhagen again, and my old home at Havndal. That's a village on the east coast, directly across the Kattegat from Halmstad, in Sweden. The day before I left the people here gave me a big *tamaara*, a native feast, and they were all on hand to see me leave by Tihoti's schooner. I kissed my old woman and the kids and off I went; but when I got to the island where I was to catch the steamer for Europe, via Panama, I found I wasn't nearly so homesick for Denmark as I was to come back here. So back I came. I'm as bad as Father Vincent. I guess the pair of us are more native than the natives themselves."

"How do they feel about Boyle?" I asked. "I don't understand their position here with him owning the island, as you say."

"It hasn't made a particle of difference," said Viggo.

"Don't they resent his ownership? Couldn't he clear them out if he wanted to?"

"Well, yes, I suppose he's got the legal right, but he'd never be foolish enough to try it. The natives never think of the island as belonging to him. It's theirs and always has been theirs, and Boyle knows it. About all his ownership means is that he's in a kind of partnership with them in the copra and pearl-shell business. He markets the produce and gets half the profit. Their half is enough for what they want to buy: a little rice and flour and tinned beef and what clothes and other things they need. So the arrangement suits them all right."

"I wonder how they'll take the idea of a base being made here?" I asked.

"Oh, you needn't worry about that," said Viggo. "I've already told them about the ship that's coming. They're as pleased as a lot of children when you promise them a picnic. It will be a big event out here. You know, there's never been a big ship called at any of these islands; they've never even seen a steamship. You can guess what a lot of excitement that will make."

I was on the point, then, of giving Viggo the facts; of making a clean breast of the real nature of the task I had come to perform. I wanted his advice as to how and when I should tell Father Vincent. But something in his happy reposeful attitude prevented me. "No!" I thought. "There's a fortnight remaining before the ship can come. Let them all have the full good of it. I'm not going to speak until I must."

Mrs. Viggo now had supper on the table. The midday meal would easily have carried me through till the next morning; nevertheless, I drew up with Viggo and made a pretense of eating. He had appetite enough for the pair of us. When we had finished we strolled across the islet to the outer beach.

"We'll go along to see the Lehmanns in an hour or

so," said Viggo. "Father Vincent and Tihoti are coming too."

"Where do they live?" I asked.

"On that *motu* just across the passage. It's the prettiest little place, not more than two hundred yards across either way, and Ruth and her father keep it as neat as a pin. Mr. Lehmann told me that if he knew he could never set foot off it for the rest of his life he'd be perfectly content. They've got a home at last, Mr. Dodd, after all the misery they've been through. I doubt if you could find two people in the whole world who would appreciate it more."

He led the way to a kind of knoll shaded by two old trees with a bench between them. It was not twenty feet above sea level, but Viggo said it was the highest spot in the circumference of the atoll.

"This is my private observation spot," he said. "It's a fine place to sit when you want to be alone."

Viggo was a comfortable companion, the kind to enjoy long silences with. He loved to talk and always had something interesting to say, but he took for granted what most men have forgotten: that silence is an essential part of conversation. He was a great reader, and I discovered that he had a wide knowledge of natural history gained through both reading and observation. As for the latter, his senses were as keen as those of a boy. Nothing escaped him.

We must have sat for a good quarter of an hour

without exchanging a word. Finally he said: "Mr. Dodd, have you ever thought what a wonder it is that human beings ever reached these islands?"

"I was thinking of it during my walk this afternoon," I replied. "Where could they have come from in the first place, and how did they get here?"

"There's a difference of opinion about that," said Viggo. "I'm no scholar. I don't claim to know much about it, but I've read what I could get my hands on about the old Polynesian migrations. Some say there never were any migrations; that these scattered islands are all that remain of a great continent that sank into the sea ages ago. Others believe no such continent existed and that the first people must have come from the east, from South America. Neither of these opinions is given much credit in these days. All the evidence goes to show that the first inhabitants must have come from the west; the finest part of them from India, in the first place."

"Is anything known of the time of their coming?" I asked.

"Here? Yes, the scholars have got a kind of a hazy notion from studying the native legends and the old genealogies, but they don't agree about the time. Some believe they came as early as the ninth century; others think it was somewhere between the tenth and twelfth."

"How did they come? In canoes?"

"Yes; in big seagoing canoes that would hold up to a hundred people, some of them. They had both single canoes with a huge outrigger, and double canoes lashed together with a platform between. But 'canoe' is hardly the word for those old ships. They were deep and broad-beamed and decked over, and could stand a lot of sea."

"There must have been scores lost for every one that reached any land," I remarked.

Viggo nodded.

"I suppose they set out in fleets, a dozen or two together, spreading out in a wide arc so as to cover as much sea as possible, keeping in touch as well as they could, at night, by blowing their conch-shell trumpets. . . . There would have been a sight to see, Mr. Dodd: a fleet of those great canoes with their matting sails, filled with men, women, and children, their pigs and fowls and dogs, nothing but empty unknown sea around them. And maybe one, the last of them all, reaching such an island as this, only a handful of people left in it, half dead from thirst and starvation."

"They must have been a hardy, courageous lot," I remarked.

"I'll tell you what I think. They've never been given half the credit due them. Long before Columbus was born some of those ancient Polynesian explorers had gone on voyages probably as long as his."

We returned across the *motu* by way of Father Vincent's house where he and the captain were waiting; then the four of us passed through the village to the beach where we took a canoe to cross the passage to the islet where the Lehmanns lived. I confess that I was none too happy in the prospect of this visit. I felt a most unreasonable irritation as well, as though it were the Lehmanns' fault for being on the island, adding another to the problems awaiting me; but that feeling vanished from the moment of our meeting.

We went ashore in a little half-moon cove where overhanging trees cast a pool of deep shadow on the starlit water. About twenty paces distant stood the house, a one-story frame dwelling facing the lagoon, with a deep veranda running the full length of it, and lighted now by a single shaded lamp throwing a mellow radiance into the night. Masses of shrubbery grew on either side of the entrance. The veranda was a charming out-of-doors living room comfortably furnished with easy chairs, tables, and settees. Open bookshelves filled with well-worn volumes formed the greater part of the back wall, and in a recess at one end stood the Bechstein piano.

Miss Lehmann was waiting at the top of the steps to greet us. Viggo and the captain had called her a beautiful girl, and she was that, certainly. She was a brunette, with thick, wavy brown hair, and her dark eyes were full of life and intelligence. She had a low voice, very agreeable to the ear, and she spoke English without a trace of accent. As Viggo introduced me and she took my hand in a firm, friendly clasp, I recalled what Father Vincent had said of her during our talk that afternoon in his garden: "She has true nobility of character, Mr. Dodd. That was my first impression of her and I think it will be yours." Viggo had told me that she was not yet twenty, but she seemed older than that, more mature than her years warranted. Her attitude toward her father had in it a touching, protective quality as though she were daughter and mother combined.

Mr. Lehmann was a man of about my own age, tall and extremely thin, with a pale sensitive face that showed no trace of Jewish blood; in fact, neither father nor daughter looked Jewish. He spoke English brokenly, with a pronounced accent, and when the greetings were over seemed well content to let his daughter do the talking for both of them. I noticed that his glance rested upon her again and again, with a kind of sad-eyed wonderment, as though he could scarcely believe that this lovely girl with her abundant vitality was his own flesh and blood; or it may have been wonder mingled with a feeling of deep gratitude that the two of them had survived to reach such a haven as this.

I was aware at once of the easy friendly relationship that had sprung up between the three old islanders and these homeless ones who had found here so happy a home. Captain George could scarcely take his eyes off Miss Lehmann. There was something comical between his habitual glare, with its false impression of hostility, and the Old World courtliness of his manner toward her. She must have found him an alarming figure at first, before she could realize how mistaken one's earliest impression of the captain was.

"Mr. Dodd," the captain was saying, "I wish you could have seen this little island before Miss Lehmann took it in hand. What a wilderness! And look at it now!"

"How can you speak of it, Tihoti," said Miss Lehmann. "It was heaven before, and it always will be heaven, to us. Father and I do no more than sweep the golden sands."

"Viggo, what do you say to that, you and Father Vincent?"

"That's right," said Viggo; "it was a regular jungle, old coconut fronds lying so deep everywhere you could hardly get through them. Father Vincent and I have our work cut out for us these days. We're both cranks about neatness and order, but my goodness! We can't keep up with Ruth, not even with the whole village to help."

I didn't know what the Lehmanns thought of my presence there. Now and then I observed Miss Lehmann's glance resting upon me in a grave questioning manner. Not a word was said of the war, or the reason for my coming, but Viggo told me, later, that he had explained to them about the ship that was on the way. "I believe that kind of scared them," he said. "They had such a terrible time in Europe they can't believe they're safe anywhere. They're always afraid something more is going to happen. But I told them they needn't worry; there'd be no Huns coming to chase them away from here."

When we had chatted for a little while, the captain took the occasion to say: "Miss Lehmann, could we have some music?"

"Of course," she said. "What would you like?"

"There's nothing you might play or sing that we wouldn't like," said George.

"Father Vincent, have you any suggestions?"

"I have indeed," he replied: "the sonata for violin and piano that you played when we were last here."

At the mention of music, Mr. Lehmann was immediately interested.

"We shall be very pleased to play it for you again, Father Vincent," he said. "We love it, too. It is Mozart's first sonata in A Major. It is strange: that sonata is not often played, but I think it is one of his best."

I am among the tens of thousands of Americans whose musical education, such as it is, has been largely self-acquired, by means of the phonograph and the radio. My mother loved the piano and played very well, but she died when I was still a youngster. After that, music formed no part of my life until the time when the phonograph was brought to its perfection as a recording instrument; then my love for it was re-awakened, and the phonograph has been my great resource ever since. It is one product of the Machine Age that compensates for many another of more than doubtful value.

And so I was able to listen with deep pleasure while Miss Lehmann and her father played, entirely from memory, the Mozart sonata. I doubt whether, in the whole world, a more perfect spot could be found for the enjoyment of music. It seemed to have been fashioned by Nature for just that kind of enjoyment.

When Boyle had bought the piano from the Russians, he also bought their library of music, a great boon to them, Miss Lehmann said, but it struck me that they would have been at no serious loss without it, for their memory was stored with music which they played without reference to the score.

That was a memorable evening to me, and the happiest part of it began when Viggo said: "Now, Ruth, let's have some of the good old songs." His first request was "Solveig's Song"; then the captain asked for "The Last Rose of Summer." Miss Lehmann had a lovely voice, clear and true and effortless. I've got a lot of sentiment in me, beneath the engineer's disguise. I soon discovered that I had a pair of blood brothers in this, in Viggo and the captain. I'm far from sure that Father Vincent was not another; at any rate, he was the very picture of contentment as he listened. Presently Miss Lehmann turned to say: "Mr. Dodd, what shall I sing for you; especially for you?" I had so many suggestions that I didn't know which to mention first, and while I was hesitating she said: "I believe I can guess one of them without your telling me. You must have English words for this, but I know only the German."

Then, to my astonishment and delight, she sang "Last Night the Nightingale Woke Me," my mother's favorite song. How often I had heard her sing it on beautiful summer nights when the whippoorwills were calling in the wood lot back of our house and the moon was rising over the hill beyond. All through boyhood nightingales meant whippoorwills to me. That hit me right where I live. Old memories came thronging back, and when Miss Lehmann had finished I paid her the furtive tribute of a tear or two.

It was past midnight when we came away. As we were paddling back to the village islet, Father Vincent remarked: "Think of the stupidity of the Germans, to call it nothing else, in driving such people from their homelands." We were silent after that. We were thinking, all of us, I believe, of the tens, the hundreds of thousands who were unable to escape the butchers; who had been driven not into exile but the grave.

The songs Miss Lehmann had sung for us stirred up such a throng of old memories and associations that I was far from sleepy when I returned to my room at Viggo's house. I was looking over a shelf of books he had there when I came upon a thin volume in paper covers: *The Worship of Kiho-Tumu*, the one Father Vincent had spoken of that afternoon. With a lamp at my elbow, I sat down to glance through it, convinced that such a book would be certain to bring on drowsiness before I had read a quarter of an hour.

I was greatly mistaken. I did more than glance: I read, my interest deepening with every page. I was astonished by what I found there. I want to read you one of the sacred chants I found in it, the translation, of course. I made a copy of it that same night, and I've carried it with me ever since. It is called: "The Song of the Exalted Presence of Kiho-the-All-Source

Concerning His Will to Bring Space and the Universe into Existence."

The Primal Source thrusts outward, upward.
The First Source of Chaos and the Night dwelling below
 in Havaiki sends forth a first pulsation of motion.
Unseen, invisible in the fathomless abyss of Night;
Sleeping face downward in the Wide-Highways-of-Repose-of-Space;
Propped on an elbow in the sunless Deep . . .
> Up, on my knees!
> Now, with bended back!
Heaving upward, I stand on Havaiki,
Erect at last upon the Sacred Mound of My Temple,
Ahu-Toru, Altar-of-Ascending-Fire,
As I will the prodigious travail of the Spheres.

> O, Majesty! O, Divinity!
> Now dreams . . .

Now dreams the Almighty God.
Now the Almighty-God-of-the-Cosmic-Night dwelling below in Havaiki, visions:
The creation of the Spirit World, an abiding place for the spirits of the dead;
The unfolding of the wide realms of the Earth, a sanctuary for the living;
The under-propping of the Sky World here above, a Homeland for the Gods;
That these multitudes reflect upon the Supreme Creator dwelling below in far Havaiki;

That they lift on high their voices in acclaim of the Source-of-All.
In Him alone is the power to perform these mighty deeds.

> O, Majesty! O, Divinity!
> These mighty deeds . . .

These mighty deeds are destined to be performed by the Creator of the Gods alone, the God Supreme!
He is the Source who shall take life away,
> That the elementals shall know,
> That the dead shall remember,
> That the living shall not forget
> (Whilst the lesser Gods acclaim me),

That I Myself am the author of these mighty deeds;
That, knowing this, the Universe proclaim
Me, Myself, the Cause-of-All.
I recline upon My Temple, Sacred-Altar-of-Ascending-Fire,
> While the fire leaps upward in streaming flame.

I was deeply impressed by this and other chants from the Kiho worship, recorded as they came from the lips of the old Polynesian of a former age. I found myself comparing "Up, on my knees! Now, with bended back!" with "And God said, 'Let there be light,' and there was light," of our own sacred writings. As a concept of the Creator in the agony of creation, the heathen one seemed to me immeasurably the more vivid.

V

Early next morning I set out with Viggo and a dozen of the natives to make a circuit of the atoll from inside of the lagoon. We were to spend the night on the turtle *motu* diagonally across the lagoon, ten miles from the village. I felt that Viggo was on pins and needles to reach this islet. He was afraid the last of the pits of turtle eggs might hatch before we could get there. However, he was very considerate. Knowing that I wanted to see all the *motu* along that far side, he suggested that we take them in on the way.

It was a glorious day, with clear skies and the wind blowing fresh from the southeast. We skimmed along at between twelve and fourteen knots, according to Viggo's estimation. He told me that such a canoe would easily do sixteen in a strong wind. His two sons managed the big steering paddle and the other fellows watched the trim. As the gusts heeled us down they would leap to a kind of runway built across the hull to the outrigger, to offset the pull of the sail. Sometimes the gusts were too quick for them; the outrigger would leap clear of the water and come smacking down again; I thought half a dozen times that we were about to capsize. On the other tack the men would bunch on the runway to the hull side to prevent the outrigger from being buried in its turn.

We went first to an islet almost in the center of the lagoon, six miles from the village. It was not more than twenty paces across; with its clumps of green scrub and a few old trees that seemed to be growing there as perches for sea birds, it made as pretty a picture as one could wish to see. We dropped the sail here and the canoe was sculled slowly around the islet to give me a view of the steep walls of coral falling away to the depths of the lagoon. I'd no idea, before, that there were so many kinds of corals, of such fantastic shapes and colors. Viggo had a small box, open on one side, the bottom covered with a watertight pane of clear glass. Set upon the water with the pane side down, it takes off the glare from the surface and you look into the depths as though you were looking through an open window. Shafts of sunlight lit up ravines and caverns far below where fishes as gorgeously colored as the corals themselves were hovering along the steep walls in countless numbers. You can imagine how the sight would appeal to a Middle Westerner used to ponds and streams so muddy you can scarcely see your hand held six inches below the surface of the water. I would have been content to stay there for the rest of the day, looking through the water-glass window. Viggo told me that the atoll was one of the best in that part of the Pacific for pearl oysters.

"I suppose that's why Boyle wanted it," he said. "He's made a pile of money from pearls and pearl shell, but the market's gone for pearls, since the war."

He asked two of the boys to give me a demonstration of how the diving is done. They trussed up their waistcloths in the fashion of swimming trunks and over the side they went. Meanwhile, Viggo attached a line to the handle of a bucket and let it down till it rested on a ledge of coral far below. The two men, holding to the side of the canoe, breathed deeply for half a minute or so, filling their lungs again and again, then they went down. Viggo had let out a hundred feet of line, but I could still see the bucket and the forms of the men diving toward it with the fish streaking on either side as they descended. From above one had the illusion that they were being splashed away by the divers, and they moved with such lightning speed they were mere streaks of brilliant color in the shafts of sunlight. The men walked, so to speak, along the coral walls far below, using both hands and feet. Pearl oysters grew thickly there and the bucket was soon filled; then with a light spring the divers rose toward the surface, their arms pressed closely to their sides, their faces turned upward. I timed the dive. One man was under water a minute and thirty-five, the other a minute and forty-eight seconds. Viggo told me that dives from two minutes to two minutes and twenty seconds were common, and that three minutes was the longest one he had ever timed. He also told me that he had known divers to go as deep as thirty fathoms but that they could not work at such a depth.

We sailed along the far side of the lagoon, making short boards away and back again so that I could examine every *motu* along the whole extent of the reef from the northwest to the far southeast end of the atoll. There were twenty-three in all, most of them tiny islets of no more than two or three acres. The largest was about a quarter of a mile from end to end and well planted to coconut palms. I saw that it would be large enough, but no more than that, to accommodate the people when the time came to shift them from the village islet.

We reached the turtle islet a little before sunset and Viggo hurried away at once to see whether or not the turtles had hatched. He returned a few minutes later, his broad face beaming.

"We're in time," he announced. "It will be tomorrow, almost certain."

"How can you tell?" I asked.

"The eggs hatch in seventy-five days. If I know when they're laid I make a record of it, but the old lady who left this lot didn't let me know about it in advance. But the hermit crabs are gathering round and that's a sure sign it won't be long."

This was the kind of islet a small boy dreams about without really believing in its existence. The beach on the lagoon side was of pure coral sand, pale gold in the westering light, and marked with the prints of sea birds' feet and the wavering tracks of hermit crabs. The seaward reef was fifty or sixty yards across, dotted with broad salt-water pools that were mirrors for the evening sky. On the landward side of it was a great rampart of coral fragments torn from the reef and heaped up there by the storms of past generations. Viggo and I seated ourselves on this rampart to watch the others spearing fish; meanwhile, two of the men had gone along the reef to another *motu*, all but joining this one, for sea birds' eggs.

The bird islet was a fascinating sight at this hour of the evening. High above it, so high that one could scarcely see them, the frigate birds were patrolling singly or in small squadrons, awaiting the return from fishing of the respectable, hard-working members of the bird community. The gannets appear to be their favorite victims. When the frigate birds spy one or two or half a dozen gannets coming in from sea, they go down in power dives that would make Jimmy Doolittle envious. The gannets are superb fliers, but so are the frigate birds, and these latter are fighters. The gannets are so many feathered Daladiers and Neville Chamberlains: peace in their time appears to be the idea with them. When hard-pressed they give a disgorging squawk and up comes the gulletful of small fish they were so hopefully carrying home to their young. The frigates dive for the spoil and seize it in midair.

When we had finished our supper of broiled fish and roasted birds' eggs, Viggo and I strolled to the place where the turtle eggs had been laid, a scarcely perceptible mound that I would not have noticed if he had not pointed it out. A score or two of hermit crabs had collected there as though waiting for something to happen. These crabs are small creatures that make their homes, as you probably know, in discarded snail shells. The full-grown crab manages to thrust his unprotected rear end into a shell about the size of your fist. They all snapped into their shells as well as they could, at our approach, and lay still. Viggo gathered them up, two or three at a time, and threw them to a good distance.

"That won't hurt 'em," he said. "I've got a kind of liking for hermit crabs. They're such harmless creatures, usually, feeding on pandanus nuts and the like of that. But they can't resist baby turtle. Blessed if I know how they can tell when the eggs are going to hatch. I think they must smell 'em. They're always on hand a little while before the turtles come out."

We seated ourselves near by at a spot where we had a clear view of the adjacent bird islet. Beyond it the reef curved away to the northwest and disappeared over the slope of the world. Thousands of birds were still in the air, flying idly back and forth in the last faint light. They seem to enjoy the day's end as much as humans do. Viggo broke a long silence to remark: —

"I wish you could be here in December, Mr. Dodd, to see the big turtle come ashore to lay their eggs."

"Do many come?" I asked.

"Not so many as there used to be; they're getting scarcer all the time. They're having as hard a struggle as the whales, these days. You know what's happened to the whales? Their last refuge was in the Antarctic. The Japs and the Norwegians have about wiped out what's left of them even there, with their big ships and modern methods of killing. This war's had at least one good effect: it's stopped the slaughter of whales, for a while, anyway."

"Are sea turtle hunted commercially?" I asked.

"Yes, but not so much in this part of the Pacific. The great trouble for them is that there are so few places, nowadays, where they can find a safe refuge for egg laying. But this *motu* is one. I see to that. I'm as partial to a fine turtle steak as any of the natives, but I've come to realize that watching them is a hundred times better than eating them. They start coming in around October, but November and December are the big months. I've seen as many as three huge turtle come ashore on the same night."

"Aren't they shy about being seen?"

Viggo didn't appear to have heard me. Presently he asked: "Excuse me, what was it you said?"

"Aren't the turtle afraid of being seen?"

"I was thinking of the strange feeling it gives you to come face to face with a big sea turtle at night, in such a lonely place as this," he replied. "And some of them *are* big: they'll weigh three, four, up to five hundred pounds and they look as old as time. . . . No, I can't say that they show any fear, but I'm always careful not to disturb them. Once a mother turtle starts digging the pit for her eggs she goes right on with her work. I've watched by moonlight and starlight. You can sit within three paces, in plain view, and she pays no more attention than she would to a bush or tree. On dark nights I've lit my lantern and set it close by. When she sees the light she halts for a bit and turns her head slowly in your direction; and that's when the queer feeling I spoke of comes over you. I don't know how to describe it. It's like . . . it's like . . . I don't know *what* it's like. You want to get up very quietly and go away. You know you have no business to be watching.

"But if you stay where you are, she soon forgets about you and goes on with her digging, using her hind flippers, first one, then the other. She digs the hole as deep as she can, say around eighteen or twenty inches, then in go the eggs, all the way from a hundred and fifty to two hundred and fifty — even more. She uses both flippers to cover the hole, patting down the sand and pressing it under her shell till she has made a good workmanlike job of it. Then she uses her powerful front flippers for the first time, scattering sand and gravel in every direction. I suppose the idea is to try and hide the place where the eggs are. She seems to forget the track she's made leading to it, and the one she'll make back to the sea."

Viggo broke off, and was so long silent that I took the occasion to say: "What happens next?"

"Mr. Dodd," he said, "it would be worth your while to come all the way back here some day to see the whole business from beginning to end. It really would. I don't know but what the most interesting part is when the old mother turtle is resting for a bit before she goes back to the sea. After watching and studying them for so long I've come to believe that turtles have a kind of sad wisdom. It stands to reason they should have when you remember how long they live, if they're given a chance to live. They're acquainted with grief, as the Bible says, especially with regard to their young ones.

"There's the tragedy. Of all the two or three hundred baby turtle that will come out of that pit in the sand, probably not a dozen will live through the dangers they'll have to meet while they're little and defenseless. I more than half believe the mother knows this. When she's resting beside the hole filled with the eggs she's tucked in and covered so nicely, you'd say she was thinking sadly about the future. A turtle has a curious hoarse way of breathing. All of a sudden she will let out a sigh it startles you to hear. It's as if she were thinking: 'I know what's to come, but there's nothing I can do about it . . . Nothing.' Then, without even a glance in your direction, she starts slowly back to sea."

"Have baby turtle so many enemies?" I asked.

"Enemies! They have nothing but enemies! Maybe you'll have a chance to see for yourself. When you remember that a mother lays two batches of eggs a year, probably four or five hundred in all, and how few grown turtle there are . . . yes, you may well say they have a hard struggle to survive. And if human beings grab every lonely sandbank that's left in the

Pacific, as they seem to be doing these days, it will mean the end of the sea turtle."

I don't know what prompted me to speak out at that moment. A sense of guilt, perhaps; the need to confess and get it over with. However that may be, I gathered up my resolution and told Viggo why I had come and what the making of a military and naval base would mean to that lonely atoll. I made no attempt to soften the blow. By the time I had finished he knew the whole desolate truth. He heard me through in silence, and the silence that followed was the only possible comment.

But at last he exclaimed, in a low voice: "Oh dear! . . . Oh dear! . . . Oh dear!"

I would not have believed that this mildest of exclamations could contain such genuine anguish of mind and heart. I managed to say: "Never in my life have I had so hateful a task to perform," and little consolation that could have been.

"Will . . . will my turtle *motu* have to go?"

"I don't know," I replied, "but you must be prepared for it. The freighter that's coming will bring a naval engineer who will decide where the various installations are to be placed. There will be anti-aircraft guns on various islets around the lagoon, that is certain. This may be one of them. . . . How will the people take this when they know the full truth?"

"It will be hard on the older ones."

"Will you be able to make them see the necessity? Can you explain what the United Nations are fighting for, and how their own welfare is concerned here?"

"Yes, in a way . . . but . . ."

"But, what?"

"You must remember, Mr. Dodd, how cut off they are from the rest of the world. The only book they have in their own language is the Bible. They know it from end to end, much better than most white people, but that's all their reading. You can't expect them to have any clear notion about the war and the countries outside. I've shown them pictures now and again of towns and great cities and railroads and tall buildings and the like of that. It don't interest them much. It's all too strange and different from their own kind of life. Someone's sure to say: 'Where's the lagoon?' or 'Where's the reef?' I've found it's useless trying to explain what a continent is.

"Then there's another thing. They have a love for their islands that goes deep down. They love every inch of ground, every little *motu* along the reefs, no matter how small. You'd have to live here and know the natives to realize how great that love is. Having so little land, it's very precious to them."

"Yes, I can well understand that."

"Well, when they see what's going to happen now,

they'll ask me questions I'll have a hard time answering. They will say: 'Viggo, you and Father Vincent have told us about the Germans and Japanese and what they would do to our islands if they had a chance to come here. But see what the friendly nations have done! How are we going to live?' What can I say, Mr. Dodd? It won't be a fair question, but how can I explain?"

I had no suggestions to make. I didn't see how it *could* be explained.

"I'm not worrying so much about the young people," he added, bleakly. "They will be so interested in what happens after the ship comes they won't think of anything else, at first. But it will be a terrible blow for the older people. . . . Then there's Father Vincent, and the Lehmanns. There's no way, you think, of saving the father's church and his garden?"

"No. They will have to go. As for the Lehmanns . . ."

I didn't complete the sentence. Old Boyle's words came back to me: "When I sent 'em out there I thought I was doing a good turn for once in my life. Guess I was too late makin' a start." I could not summon up even a bitter smile as I thought of the irony of the situation as it applied to the Lehmanns. Where on this tormented planet could a refuge be found if not here? But my one meeting with them was enough to convince me that they would take this new development with the stoicism they had learned from hard experience.

"When did they come?" I asked.

"The Lehmanns? Eight months ago. In July, last year."

"They've had that, at least."

"Yes," said Viggo.

He sat with his chin in his hands, his elbows propped on his broad knees, gazing at the path of glory in the lagoon made by the first-quarter moon, now low in the west. Presently he said: "Mr. Dodd, here's what I suggest. A week from tonight the people will have one of their *himinés;* it's a kind of song service. Every now and then they get together to sing their old songs that have been handed down from generation to generation. I think you'd enjoy hearing them."

"I certainly would," I replied.

"Well, I'll say nothing till that's over. I can tell them that same night, after the singing. They'll all be together then."

"Good," I said, "it's an excellent suggestion."

The moon had set when we returned to the place where the camp had been made. Viggo's sons and the other men had spread the sail of the canoe for their own bed. Mats with pillows and coverlets Viggo had brought were laid out for us. I was impressed by the prayer service in progress as we came in. All those young fellows took part in it with a complete lack of self-consciousness. They were repeating prayers of the Catholic Church, but there was nothing perfunctory in their manner of doing so. The loneliness of the place, with the empty sea around and the great vault of sky, spangled with stars, overhead, gave a peculiar solemnity to that brief evening service. I felt that worship meant something to these people; that it was a necessary part of their daily lives.

I couldn't go to sleep for a long time, and, although we had no further conversation, I knew that Viggo was as wakeful as myself. But at last I heard his measured breathing, with intervals of snoring between. I lay on my back staring into the sky. In those Southern latitudes, with no human lights, or dust, or smoke to obscure the view, the vast arc of Milky Way is of awe-inspiring splendor. I felt that I had never before really seen the Milky Way, but what chance do most of us Northerners, city dwellers, give ourselves to see it? Near the constellation of the Southern Cross is that abyss of blackness so inadequately named "the Coal Sack," opening into ancient and eternal Night. I thought I heard a chorus of mocking voices — the Ironic Spirits of Thomas Hardy's "Dynasts" — issuing from the void: —

    Pour all your troubles down the old Coal Sack
    And smile, smile, smile.

But I lack the cosmic point of view. Human concerns are all-important to me, so I was not comforted.

VI

NEXT MORNING THE TURTLES hatched out. I'm tempted to give you a full account of that, but it's something to see rather than to hear about. One of Viggo's boys came to wake me. He spoke no English, but his gestures were eloquent; I knew at once what was happening and hurried after him to the seaward side of the *motu*. The others were already on hand, and there was Viggo, rushing up and down the beach from the turtle pit to the reef, waving an old brown coconut frond over his head to scare the birds away. And down from the pit, about fifty yards inland, came a thin line of baby turtle, each of them about the size of an American half-dollar, scurrying toward the sea as fast as their tiny flippers would carry them. They could walk and swim from the moment of birth, but otherwise they were as helpless as newly born human infants.

"Excuse me for waking you up, Mr. Dodd," said Viggo, "but I thought you'd want to see this."

"I certainly do," I replied, and, in fact, I wouldn't have missed the strange sight for anything. But I was fully as interested in watching Viggo as I was in the turtle. He might have been old Father Turtle himself, trying his best to protect his host of harassed children as they made toward the sea. The birds hovered above them in clouds, and despite all that Viggo and the boys, under his direction, could do to keep them off, they would swoop down and seize the tiny defenseless creatures. Viggo would gather up a hatful and hurry down with them to the water, but he had even less chance to protect them there than before: the fish were as eager for those tender morsels as the birds.

The surf was thundering over the wide reef, flooding the pools and channels in the coral, and the spume thrown high filled the air with a perpetual cloud of rainbow-colored mist.

"There she is, Mr. Dodd!" said Viggo, pointing to a wide pool in the reef, a good forty yards out. "You see her?"

"Who?" I asked.

"The old mother turtle. She must have come in last night."

I was incredulous.

"You tell me she knows when her eggs will hatch?" I asked.

"My goodness! Why shouldn't she? Of course she knows! This isn't the first time I've seen it happen. . . . Look! . . . There! You see her splashing? It's like she was saying: 'Hurry, children! Here's your mother!'" and away he went again, waving his palm frond. He had completely forgotten, for the moment at least, the sorrow to come.

For all his efforts and those of the native boys, there was a woeful slaughter of baby turtle that morning. I could see the fish streaking across the shallows after those that had succeeded in reaching the water. Presently Viggo came back to where I was standing. He was puffing and blowing, and although the sun was not yet an hour high, his shirt and trousers were soaked with sweat.

"I expect you think I'm an awful fool," he said, with an apologetic smile.

"Not in the least," I replied, "but it does seem hopeless, trying to save them."

He nodded, glumly.

"You see now what I meant when I spoke about their enemies? I don't suppose more than thirty or forty of the whole lot will live to reach the sea, if that many. And the danger isn't over then. Far from it!"

He told me he had a pen fenced off in the shallows of the lagoon where he raised many baby turtle until their shells had hardened and they were able to fend for themselves; then he let them go. "It's a nice hobby," he said. "I certainly enjoy it." Of a sudden he remembered, and I shall not soon forget the expression that came over his face as he added: "But I don't suppose I'll be able to do it any more, after the ship comes."

"Remember, Viggo; this is only for the duration of the war," I said.

"I know . . . there's that to think of." He shook his head, slowly. "But I'm afraid it will never again be like it is now . . . Well, we can hope, anyway."

We spent the day and the following night on the turtle islet. The experience gave me the true "feel," so to speak, of Low Island life. I could imagine this sort of thing going on year after year, generation after generation. Those native boys were as much a part of the natural history of the place as the sea fowl, the hermit crabs, the turtle and the fish. They belonged there. They had been molded by the environment into as fine a type of primitive man as, I believe, could be found anywhere. I don't like the word "primitive," in this connection, with its connotation of slow wits and darkened minds. Slow-witted they certainly were not. Their minds were, no doubt, dark in the sense that they contained little knowledge except that useful to them in their daily lives; but how wide that knowledge was I had occasion to observe at all hours. I was the dark-minded, slow-witted one here. My ignorance of their kind of knowledge was abysmal.

It was a treat to see their "at-homeness" whether on land, on the reef, or in the sea. Viggo kept a small outrigger canoe on this *motu*. He thought it would interest me to see how they spear fish in the sea beyond the reef, and I willingly accepted the chance. The canoe — large enough for four occupants — was carried to a place fairly free from the villainous knife-edged coral that covered much of the reef. Here we embarked, Viggo, two of the boys, and myself, and the canoe was paddled through the broken water foaming across the reef to a V-shaped opening on the seaward side where it could easily be launched despite the surf. At least, so Viggo said, but as I watched the combers piling in I didn't see how it was to be done. At the moment I would gladly have renigged this expedition planned for my benefit, but pride wouldn't allow me to. So I sat fast and waited, taking heart from the expressions of complete assurance on the faces of the others.

Two men held the canoe while the seas piled in, and when the precise moment came Viggo shouted an order. We were given a shove; the paddlers pulled with quick hard strokes, and we shot out toward the long steepening slope of a comber sweeping majestically in to break on the reef. Up and over it we went, and thirty seconds later we were riding easily over the swells past all danger. I learned anew from that experience how readily old Mother Ocean — sometimes, at least — will aid the purposes of men. But there's no sentiment about her. Meet her conditions and thrive. Fail to meet them and suffer the consequences.

Meanwhile, here came the fish spearers. They swam out through the surf, trailing their slender, single-pronged spears which they clasped with their toes. Imagine one of us trying to clasp anything with his toes, least of all while swimming through a heavy surf!

The canoe was paddled slowly along a little way beyond the break of the seas, while the spearers were at work. I couldn't see them well at that distance, but I caught an occasional glimpse as they went down toward the steeply sloping wall of the reef. Then a head would break water, the diver now holding his spear upright, sometimes with two fish impaled, one above the other. They pulled them off on the sides of the canoe and down they would go again. They wore homemade diving goggles that gave them an odd scholarly look, and scholars they were at that business: they could read a coral reef, and come away with their knowledge of it impaled on the point of a fishing spear. They were piscatorial Ph.D.'s and Litt.D.'s.

That was a memorable experience for me, but I was relieved when we were safely over the reef again. The coming in was as beautifully timed and as neatly done as the going out. I saw that anyone could do this kind of thing as easily as breathing, even the fishing part of it, if his ancestors had been Low Islanders for several centuries.

I felt that I was getting to be a pretty good amateur Low Islander, so when we had crossed the outer ledge of reef I got out of the canoe to walk across the shallows to the beach. The water was no more than thigh deep.

"Look out for the sea urchins," Viggo warned. He had already spoken of these; you see them everywhere on the reefs. They are beautiful things to look at, of a deep shade of blue or purple, covered with long needle-pointed spines that stick out on all sides. But those spines can give you a lot of grief if you chance to bash a hand or foot against them. The pain is soon relieved, Viggo said, if you apply urine to the spot; apparently the ammonia dissolves the points of the spines that break off in the wound. But I had no desire to be urinated upon so I walked warily.

I was wading slowly along, examining the strange forms of marine life, both animal and vegetable, when one of the boys who was with me grasped my arm and drew me back just as I was about to take a step. "*Nohu*," he said. That meant nothing to me. Following his glance I peered into the clear water but saw nothing there to be alarmed about. With an underhand thrust of his spear he impaled what I thought was a gorgeously colored lump of coral; but the color was the only gorgeous thing about it. It was a fish, and a more monstrous-looking thing I have never seen. You would have said that it was the embodiment of the Spirit of Evil: Schickelgruber, in the form of a fish; I was tempted to say, "*Heil*, Hitler!" Viggo had come up by this time.

"Mr. Dodd," he said, "if you had stepped on that fellow, within five minutes you would have wished you were dead. And you might have been dead before many days had passed."

He pointed out two hollow ducts in the spines of the dorsal fin.

"He lies amongst the coral with that fin erect," said Viggo. "Why, only the devil knows; and if you step on him he squirts into your foot poison that *is* poison. It's worse than any rattlesnake bite."

"Are these things common?" I asked.

"No, heaven be thanked!" said Viggo. "But you can never be sure where you will find one. They seem to take on the color of whatever part of the reef they inhabit. I've seen *nohu* with no color at all lying amongst fragments of dead coral. All that you can say for this fish is that it's very good eating."

I proved that for myself at our midday meal. It was excellent eating, and thankful I was that it was the flesh and not the poison I had partaken of that day.

We returned to the village early the next morning. With a good following breeze we fairly flew down the lagoon, covering the ten miles in forty minutes. While we were still a good distance off, Viggo, who was looking ahead, remarked: "That's strange! The schooner's gone!" He couldn't account for it. "Tihoti always stays three or four days when he calls here," he added. "He said nothing about leaving early this time."

We soon learned the reason for his going. During our absence a small cutter had arrived from an island eighty miles distant. An old woman was dying there and she had begged to have Father Vincent sent for; she could not die in peace unless he was present to perform the last rites; therefore, some members of her family had come for him. This island was dead to windward and it would have taken the cutter several days to beat up to it. The schooner, using her engine, could reach it overnight, so Captain Tihoti, with Father Vincent, set out at once. The captain was going on to the southeast, afterward, and would call for the priest on his homeward voyage.

Upon hearing this news, I confess that I had, at first, a feeling of profound relief. Chance had spared me the hateful task of telling Father Vincent what I had decided to tell him immediately upon our return to the village. But, upon reflection, I greatly regretted that I had not spoken that first afternoon when we met in his garden. Now, almost certainly, he would not return until at least a week after the arrival of the freighter. By that time . . .

"I believe it's best as it's turned out," Viggo said when I spoke of this. "Since it has to come, Mr. Dodd, I believe the father would *want* to be away, if he could. I'm glad he's not here to see what's going to happen."

"But think of his return," I said.

"I know," said Viggo, bleakly. "Well . . . there's nothing we can do about it now."

The arrival of the cutter gave me another glimpse into island life. A young native, about twenty, had taken the chance to come with it for the purpose of seeking a bride for himself. Viggo told me that this sort of thing happened often.

"The natives are very careful about inbreeding," he explained; "more careful, even, than we are: you never hear of one of them marrying a cousin. They would consider that the next thing to incest. There are not many inhabitants on any of the atolls. This one is about typical of the numbers you'll find all through the Group. So when young men are ready to get married and settle down, they often make long voyages to some other island to find a wife that has no blood relationship with their family. Sometimes they will stay on the wife's island, and sometimes they will bring their girls back to their own."

He spoke of one fellow who had come for a wife from an island at the far end of the archipelago, six hundred miles distant. Father Vincent had married the pair, and they were waiting for their first child to be born before going to the husband's island.

"They haven't long to wait," said Viggo. "The child is expected any day."

As a matter of fact, it arrived three days later. There was no physician to attend the mother, but that didn't matter. Old Papa Viggo was on hand; and every island woman of middle age or beyond has had long practice in midwifery. Later I saw this infant, a fine lusty boy. If he lived out his allotted span he would see the year 2012. I wondered, none so hopefully, what kind of Polynesia there would be at that distant date.

During that week, I was busy indoors and out.

Viggo provided me with a large table to work at, and with his data and what I myself collected, I made a large-scale map of the atoll marked with the shoals in the lagoon and every *motu* large and small on the reef. Although the final decision as to where the various buildings and other installations were to be placed rested with the naval engineer coming with the freighter, I sketched on the plan my own suggestions. I left blank Viggo's turtle refuge and the adjacent bird islet.

Viggo was worried about the burying ground. "You know, Mr. Dodd," he said: "the natives have great reverence for the dead. I don't know but what you might better call it 'fear.' If the dead are disturbed the living will suffer for it: they're as certain of that as they are of tomorrow's sunrise." I set his mind at rest about this. The cemetery was at the far end of the village *motu* near the spot where old Kamaké had his hut. It was enclosed by a low wall and there were no trees within it. The islet lay northwest and southeast, in the eye of the prevailing wind. Planes landing would skim over the cemetery, and those leaving would taxi to that end and turn into the wind just by the wall. They would have the full length of the islet — a good 2400 yards — for the takeoff, a sufficient distance even for bombing or transport planes. I assured him that the cemetery was safe, but I was not so certain of the repose of the dead, under those circumstances.

Viggo was sitting in my guest-room "office" while I worked on the map.

"I don't see how we will do for fresh water," he said, "with two or three hundred extra men here." He could scarcely believe me when I told him that we would have a distilling unit capable of furnishing six thousand gallons per day.

"My goodness! Is that so?" he exclaimed. After a long silence he added: "It's going to be terribly interesting to see all this . . . but oh dear! . . . Oh dear! . . ."

I thought "terribly interesting" just about expressed it, from Viggo's point of view.

The weather during this week was perfect, and I mean just that. Throughout the day the trade wind blew cool and fresh, tempering the midday heat. At sunset or a little after it would die away, and the reef-enclosed lagoon had the purity of stillness one sees in a mountain lake. The moon was coming on toward the full, and the shadows of the coconut fronds, of the pandanus trees with their tufts of long slender leaves, of the old pukatea trees, the patriarchs of the island, seemed to be woven into the texture of the white sand beneath them. The far-off incessant thunder of the surf along the outer reefs accentuated the peace within. It was as though the reefs were saying to the clamor coming from the outside world: "Thus far and no farther!" One soon ceased to hear, consciously, the roar of the surf. Despite it, perhaps because of it, the silence within the circle of woven sound was perfection itself.

I remember with especial pleasure an evening when Viggo, the Lehmanns, and I paddled in a canoe far out on the lagoon and then drifted. We talked little, well content to let the voices of the night speak in our stead. Now and then a sooty tern would pass high overhead uttering its curious harsh cry; it seemed to be dropping hard pellets of connected sound, making ripples in the great pool of silence. Some of the natives were line-fishing off the shoals not far from the passage. We were a good mile distant, yet we heard their voices plainly; but they too were silent for the most part. Occasionally, one of them who had a beautifully clear tenor voice would sing a little refrain and, after an interval of silence, would repeat it in another, higher key. To me it was the very voice of mid-ocean solitude. I have only to hum it to see again the island as it was that night. No one spoke of it then; no comment would have been adequate to express the effect of the refrain that seemed to come from an immeasurable distance; but three nights later, when Viggo and I went over to spend an hour with the Lehmanns, we heard it again, woven into a sonata for violin and piano. Mr. Lehmann had composed it during the interval, and I doubt whether Mozart himself could have done it more beautifully.

On the Saturday night the people gathered for the *himiné*, as they call it — the song service. It was held on an open plot of ground near Viggo's house. They brought mats to sit on and arranged themselves in a wide semicircle facing the lagoon, the view of it framed by two old trees growing on the beach. Miss Lehmann was there. I saw her chatting with some of the women as easily as though she herself were a Low Islander, but I suppose the fluency was less real than it seemed to be. In any case it was a remarkable achievement, I thought, to have learned so much of the native speech in a period of eight months. Viggo had brought out chairs for himself and me and we sat facing the others, a little to one side. He said we could best get the effect of the singing at that distance.

Presently the laughing and talking died away. An old man got up in his place and, in a simple, dignified manner, made a brief speech, addressed, apparently, to Viggo.

"It's for you," Viggo said, when he had finished. "He says you are welcome here. They are happy to learn of the great ship that is to pass this way. Now they will sing you some of their ancient songs."

"Am I supposed to reply?" I asked.

"No. When the singing is ended I will speak for you."

A moment later they began. There was no leader for the chorus; they had not even a tuning fork to give them the pitch, and needed none. Singing is their great art, perfected over the centuries, handed down from generation to generation. But how am I to describe this kind of singing? It's impossible. I can only say that it made a deep and strange impression upon me. The effect of it, heard on such a night, in such a place, was one never to be forgotten.

A woman's voice invariably opened each song. It was an extraordinary one, clear and sweet and true, with an astonishing range; the highest notes were almost beyond the reach of hearing. I tried to pick out that particular woman, but all sang with such apparent ease that I could not distinguish in the moonlight the one who carried that leading part. When I inquired of Viggo, he replied, with a pleased smile: "That's my old woman. I guess her voice is what made me a Low Islander. But she was a mighty pretty girl twenty-five years ago."

The singing continued for at least an hour and a half. During this time I felt rather than saw Viggo's increasing anxiety as the moment approached when he was to tell the people of what was to come. I felt sorry for him, sorry for Father Vincent and the Lehmanns, sorry for me, and, above all, sorry for them. It seemed to me that the impending sudden and brutal change in their lives demanded by the harsh necessity of war, to be imposed upon them whether they would or no, was a tragedy for the entire human race. We are all members of one great family, and the health of the whole comes, in part at least, from the variety of the contributions made to the sum of living. When the uniqueness and the integrity of any contribution is lost, something precious and irreplaceable has been lost forever. There was no doubt in my mind as to the value of what was about to be destroyed here. Ten days on the island had more than convinced me of its worth.

When the singing ended, Viggo got slowly to his feet and paced back and forth for a moment or two; then he turned to address them. He had acquired the same dignity and simplicity of manner in speaking which comes as second nature to the Polynesians, or he may always have possessed it. Perhaps it was both native and acquired. He was one of those men who haven't a grain of deceit in their natures; who are men of good will in the high sense. As I have said, he had a big heart — big rather than soft, filled with sympathy and compassion for others in their griefs and trials.

I could not understand his words, but knew well

enough, of course, what he was saying. Studying the faces of his audience as well as I could in the bright moonlight, I had a feeling of reassurance. They appeared to be taking in what he said very quietly, as though neither surprised nor angered. No bitter looks were cast in my direction, but Viggo, I felt certain, would explain that I was a mere agent, without responsibility in the matter, except with respect to the task I had been sent out to perform.

When he had finished, several of the older men rose, in turn, to reply briefly. Their voices, insofar as I could judge, had in them neither heat nor bitterness. Then the crowd quietly dispersed, and Viggo and I were left alone. He suggested that we go to his bench on the seaward side of the *motu*. We walked in silence and seated ourselves there. At last I was constrained to remark: "They seem to have taken it very well."

"They don't understand," he replied, sorrowfully.

"They don't understand? How is that possible?" I asked.

"Mr. Dodd, I told them just what is going to happen. I explained everything as you have explained it to me. And still they don't understand. They heard my words, but they haven't grasped the meaning of them — not yet, anyway. They're not dumb, as you might think from this. But they can't conceive of such a thing happening to their island. It doesn't make sense to them."

"I don't wonder," I replied. "It *doesn't* make sense, from any customary point of view."

"I expect we'd feel the same," said Viggo, "if strangers were to come to our own lands and tell us we must get out at once — crowd ourselves into a corner and let them have the rest to do what they pleased with. We wouldn't believe them."

"Well?" I said.

"There's nothing to be done about it. We'll have to wait and let the truth come in to them little by little. They'll realize soon enough, after the ship comes."

I left Viggo when we crossed the path leading to the church. He returned to the village. I walked on to Father Vincent's garden. In the bright moonlight both church and garden seemed enchanted places that might vanish even as I looked at them. How close that was to the truth of the matter no one knew better than myself. The place was deserted now, but that same afternoon the whole village had gathered there while Viggo divided among the children the fruit of the fine orange tree. They in turn had shared with the grownups so that there was at least a part of an orange for everyone.

Walking slowly along the paths I came to the jam-fruit tree, casting a circle of shade so deep I would not have noticed that the bench beneath it had an occupant. I stopped short as my name was called. Miss Lehmann was seated there.

"I'm still under the spell of the singing," she was saying a moment later. She spoke so quietly and calmly that at first I thought she might not have understood what Viggo had told the people.

"You've heard it before, of course?" I replied.

"Yes. I never miss the *himinés*. Usually my father comes too. Have you ever heard stranger music, Mr. Dodd? I've never seen my father so stirred as he was when we first listened to these songs. He has tried to get some of them down on paper, but he says it's impossible. It can't be done."

"He succeeded wonderfully well with the refrain we heard the fisherman sing," I replied.

"I know, but that was only a phrase, quite different from this other choral singing. Did you like what he did with it?"

"Very much," I replied. "I don't believe that Mozart or Beethoven could have bettered that sonata."

"Oh, you mustn't say that!" I could see that she was shocked by the comparison. "My father has real talent at musical composition, but he would be the first to say that it goes no farther than talent."

We fell silent. I knew that she was waiting for me

to speak first of what was in both our minds. Presently I said: "You understood, Miss Lehmann, what Viggo told the people this evening?"

She nodded, without speaking.

"I can understand what a blow this will be to you and your father."

"To us? What does it matter?" she replied, mournfully. "But the poor people . . . They haven't yet grasped the truth of it, Mr. Dodd."

"That's what Viggo told me."

"They are thinking more of the ship that's coming than of what will happen after it comes."

"What of yourself, Miss Lehmann? What will you and your father do now? What will you want to do?"

"Can you ask me that? We would like to stay, of course."

"Do you realize what we shall have to do in making a naval and military base here? The place will be stripped bare. . . . There will be nothing left but the climate," I added, grimly. "Even that will be changed with most of the trees gone."

"Stripped bare? The whole of it? How are the people to live?"

I spoke of the *motu* on the far side of the lagoon to which they would be moved. "Aside from that," I added, "I'm afraid there'll be nothing left except the bones of an atoll."

"Mr. Dodd," she said, "I believe I'm almost as sorry

for you as I am for the natives. I can see how you love the island already. To have to destroy it before you've had a chance to really know it . . ."

That was unexpected. I didn't reply for some little time; then I said: "I'm an engineer, Miss Lehmann. This kind of a job is right down my street, and I shan't have to stay here after the job is finished. Meanwhile, among other . . . among other matters, I've got to think of your and your father's situation."

I could not see her face clearly, but I thought I could detect a kind of mournful gaiety in her voice as she replied: "Why didn't you say 'problems' as you were about to do? The old problem of the Jews, individually or collectively! It gathers age with the passing of the centuries, but that is all the years bring to it. The solution is as far away as ever."

"Miss Lehmann, do you really want to stay here?"

"Of course. Where else *can* we go?"

"Then you shall," I said. "I'll take it upon myself to promise that in advance. I don't yet see how it's to be arranged, but we'll manage it."

She shook her head, slowly. "I won't have you making promises. You might be compelled to break them. When I said 'Where can we go?' I didn't really mean it. One thing Jewish refugees have learned is that, outside of Nazi-held Europe, we can, somehow, continue to exist."

"How did you manage in Portugal?"

It was a thoughtless question. I was sorry the moment I'd spoken.

"Father and I had a difficult time there because so many refugees were crowded into that small country. But . . . we did survive."

"Difficult" — I could imagine what lay behind that understatement. The Lehmanns were not the kind of people who would push themselves forward in a bitter struggle for mere existence, or make a show of wretchedness in the hope of sympathy.

"When is the ship expected?" she asked, a moment later.

"Any day, now."

She got to her feet. "Then I'm going for a walk to the end of the *motu*. Will you come? It may be the last chance to see it as it is now."

Many a young man would have envied me that experience, in that company. For all the fact that I have a son and daughter older than she, it was reassuring to find that my middle-aged heart could respond to the attraction, so unconsciously exerted, of that charming presence. However, the heart had not middle-aged for nothing. I was not even tempted to make a fool of myself.

What chiefly attracted me was the rare combination of youth and maturity of character. One felt no desire to "talk down" to her in the fashion that so often seems necessary when a man in his fifties tries to make conversation with a girl in her teens. There was a level head on those young shoulders, one filled with sad wisdom and profound common sense.

I spoke of old man Boyle, painting a somewhat flattering picture of the impression he had made upon me.

She heard me through, and then said: "Mr. Dodd, my father and I could never, never repay him for his kindness to us. But we have never before been objects of charity, and that is what our situation here amounts to. This seems a small-minded thing to say. One should be able to accept a generous gift in the same fine spirit in which it is offered; but we have our accursed pride. It's a defect in both of us, but there it is!"

I might have protested, with truth, that Boyle's obligation to them was far greater than theirs to him. What he had done for them had cost him nothing but the money involved and he was well able to afford that. His unselfish act — the only one in a lifetime, if Captain George was right about it — had, unquestionably, greatly salved his feeling of self-contempt. But I could hardly speak of this. I knew, of course, that Miss Lehmann was entirely right in thinking that Boyle had not really needed them to care for his home here. He had been under no necessity of sending all the way to Europe for assistance in that matter. So I said nothing. I hate dissimulation, even for a good purpose.

"No," she added, "much as we love the island, Father and I could not have remained indefinitely as pensioners here."

"Had you made any plans for the future?"

"Yes. At the end of the year we hoped to return to the other island, the seat of government. Father feels certain that he could find a position there, teaching violin in the schools and privately. I am a stenographer. I believe I could find work in some office, perhaps for Mr. Boyle himself."

"Are you a good stenographer?" I asked.

"Better than that — expert. I can say it without self-flattery. I type in English and French as easily as in German. I was employed in the office of the university where my father was Professor of Ancient History. I carried this work in addition to my studies there."

"In that case, I believe we can find a job for you here, if you really want to stay," I replied.

"That would suit me very well," she said, "but you're to make no promises and you're not to worry about us. Whether we stay or go, Father and I will be all right. . . . Mr. Dodd, it's heaven for us merely to breathe free air. We could live on that alone, if necessary. You'd have to be a Jew from Central Europe to realize how nearly that comes to being sober truth."

We walked slowly on to the end of the *motu*, skirting the end of it from the ocean side to the lagoon beach. Approaching old Kamaké's hut we saw him seated in bright moonlight near by, plaiting palm fronds; he was, evidently, preparing a new roof for the hut. He plaited rapidly; his old hands seemed to have lost none of their skill at that work. As we passed, Miss Lehmann greeted him with the customary "*Kia ora na*." He made no reply except to raise his head for a brief glance, as though regarding something that had neither meaning nor interest for him.

"He seems a surly old fellow," I remarked, presently. "Has he ever spoken to you?"

"Never. Father Vincent told me that he has not been able to exchange a dozen words with Kamaké in all the years he has lived here."

"How do the natives regard him?"

"With great respect, mingled with fear."

Both Miss Lehmann and her father had read Viggo's copy of *The Worship of Kiho-Tumu*, and had been as deeply impressed by it as myself.

"Think of his extraordinary memory," she said, "carrying those ancient chants, word for word, in his head all these years!"

"I'm surprised that he could have been persuaded to repeat them," I said.

"He didn't want them to be lost; that was his reason, evidently. My father says this record alone is enough to convince him of the antiquity and the high origin of the Polynesian race. No primitive island people, he thinks, could have conceived that worship of a supreme god. They must have brought it from some ancient homeland."

We passed through the burying ground, lying in full moonlight. Many of the older graves were marked only with borders of shells or coral fragments. Others had headstones of coral lime with a cross and the names and ages of those sleeping beneath. There was one larger stone over the grave of an Englishman who had died here years ago. Viggo had told me of this man. When dying he had asked to have the single word, REPOSE, carved on his tomb. The word seemed to ring soundlessly in the air of that lonely spot.

Miss Lehmann turned to me.

"Will Kamaké have to be moved from the *motu* with the others?" she asked.

"I'm afraid so," I replied. "That old tree that shades his hut will, certainly, have to go."

"I wish he was safely here," she said. "I wish he could die before the ship comes!"

VII

THAT WISH WAS NOT TO BE fulfilled. The freighter arrived thirty-six hours later. The night before she was sighted I spent alone on the small *motu* in the middle of the lagoon. I wanted a taste of complete solitude while the chance offered, so Viggo took me out there in one of the sailing canoes. I could not have chosen a better place or a better night for such an experience. My only companions were about a dozen gannets and frigate birds that made their home on the *motu*. They perched in the few low trees and bushes regarding me with a kind of watchful indifference. I was surprised to find the timid gannets hobnobbing on the same small islet with their enemies, the frigate birds. Perhaps the few I saw there were the Quislings of their species.

Presently the waning moon rose directly behind a *motu* on the far side of the lagoon, revealing its scattered coconut palms and pandanus trees in clear silhouette, at the moment of rising.

> The moving moon went up the sky,
> And nowhere did abide;
> Softly she was going up,
> And a star or two beside . . .

That is a perfect description of the night. I wish I had been able to banish the thoughts that marred the peace of it, for engineer Dodd.

Early next morning I saw the sailing canoe heading up for the *motu*. While it was still a good half-mile off I knew, by Viggo's attitude as he stood by the mast, that he was bringing news, and I had no doubt as to what it might be.

"She's in sight!" he called, as soon as they were within hailing distance. "She can't be seen yet from below, but the boys say she's coming up fast!"

For the past three days he had kept some of the youngsters on lookout in the tops of the highest coconut palms in the seaward side of the village *motu*.

I got into the canoe with the others, and with the wind abeam we made direct for the passage. The natives were as excited as Viggo himself and kept their glances fixed ahead as we passed out of the lagoon and met the long smooth swells of the open sea.

"There she is!" said Viggo, pointing out a faint smudge of smoke barely discernible on the horizon to the northwest. In their eagerness to see the ship the boys forgot to watch the trim of the canoe, and the first thing we knew the outrigger rose high in air, hung there the fraction of a second, and came smacking down again. Most of us were spilled out and the canoe was half filled with sea water. It was a merry experience; the boys laughed and shouted as Viggo came sputtering up. I don't know what he said, but it must have been something like: "My goodness! . . . You boys! . . . Ain't you got any sense? . . . Can't you watch things better'n that?" Meanwhile, he and I clung to the gunwale while they lowered the sail and bailed the canoe dry; then they hauled us in.

"We're in a fine state to meet the ship," said Viggo, with an apologetic grin. He was dressed in his best suit of white drill and his broad-brimmed Sunday hat with a narrow ribbon of black around the crown. "We can go back and change if you want to, but if we stay where we are we'll probably dry out before they get here."

I was all for the latter, so we wrung out our soppy clothing and put it on again. As a matter of fact we were all but dry when the ship was still a good mile distant.

I was puzzled by the size of her. The freighter I'd seen at the pier in Oakland, ready for cargo, was of about five thousand tons. The one approaching was twice as large. When we saw the men crowded along the bulwarks and looking down at us from every available perch on deck, Viggo said: "My goodness! Are they all coming here? There won't be standing room for so many!"

"It's not the ship I expected," I said. "There must

have been some change in plan since I left San Francisco."

"Maybe they've got more than one place to go," said Viggo, and that proved to be the truth of the matter.

Viggo took the steering paddle. The boys with us were as much concerned as himself to make a good impression upon the watchers. The ship was now approaching very slowly and a boarding ladder had been put over the side. The sail fluttered down at just the right second and we came alongside in fine style. Before Viggo and I were halfway up the ladder the canoe was away again, the sail bellying out to the breeze.

We were met at the gangway by the first mate and an officer who introduced himself as Commander Brigham of the Navy. He was the engineer I was to work with. The mate conducted Viggo to the bridge while the commander and I stood by the gangway, talking for a bit.

He was around thirty-five, a serious, intelligent-looking fellow, smartly dressed and with just the slightest touch of condescension in his manner. He was very courteous, but his manner as he introduced himself said: "Colonel Dodd? Of the National Guard, I believe? It seems that we're to work together. War makes strange bedfellows, doesn't it?"

My thought was: "I'll bet he's a first-class engineer. What does it matter if he high-hats me a bit? A temporary colonel of the National Guard doesn't have to stand on his dignity."

That short climb up the ship's side had taken me from one climate to another, from one world to another. Inwardly, I'd said good-bye to the island as I stepped out of the canoe and grasped the ropes of the boarding ladder, and I was back in the U.S.A. the moment I set foot on the freighter's deck. For all the feeling of sadness, with respect to the island, I was conscious of a pleasant, quickening sense of homecoming as I looked about me and sniffed in once more the fragrance of machinery. It does have a kind of fragrance to a man of my profession. My old engineering self reasserted its authority. I was again a man with a job to do, and here around me, stowed on deck, were the tools for the job: some in crates, some under tarpaulins, some already uncased, groomed for action the moment they should be swung over the ship's side.

The workers with these tools, young fellows most of them, were not thinking of the job at the moment. They were crowded three deep along the bulwarks, looking toward the island.

"Sure they're coconut trees! Can't you see the nuts in 'em?"

"Boy, don't that water look good! What a place to swim!"

"Oh yeah? I'll bet it's full of sharks."

"Say! Is that all the land there is? Not much room to move around."

"You don't move around on a South Sea island, you simp! You sit under a coconut tree and play a ukulele."

"Yeah, and when you get hungry you reach up and pick a banana and a coupla breadfruit."

"Hell! This ain't what I expected. I thought the islands was bigger."

"Buddy, we'll have 'em changed for you right away. Give us a little time."

It was the U.S.A. all right. There were boys of all kinds, conditions, and environments; boys silent and boys talkative; boys from the great cities, from farms and country towns; from the plains country, the timber country; from universities, high schools, trade schools, and from no schools to speak of save that of experience. Some were the kind to make the most of this sojourn in tropical seas. To others the experience would mean little or nothing and they would return home to grouse about having been buried on a lousy little island a thousand miles from nowhere. Some would lament deeply what was to be done to the island;

others would not think twice about this aspect of the situation.

Despite what Europeans say of us, we Americans are inclined to be apologetic about ourselves as a nation, and we're a mixture of all kinds, of course, good, bad, and indifferent, just as every other nation is. But as I looked over this sample of the U.S.A., this cross section of it, hastily collected for an emergency job and crowded into a 10,000-ton freighter, I felt pretty confident about the future of the country. I seemed to get a fresh and encouraging slant upon the generation just on the threshold of manhood, and I wondered whether another such shipload of young men, collected from whatever country, would have shown a higher proportion of well-shaped, well-knit bodies and alert, intelligent faces. There must have been a bewildering mixture of bloods represented here, but all these fellows looked, and were, American.

"I'd better take you along to see General Clarke," Commander Brigham was saying. "I expect he's up by now."

"There's a general aboard?" I asked.

"Three," said the commander.

I wish I could give you the precise inflection of his voice as he uttered this one word. It was the distilled essence of the U.S. Navy's feeling toward the U.S.

Army. It contained the history of all the feuds, jealousies, clashings of authority common between these branches of the Service since we have had a navy and an army. I smiled inwardly, but maintained an expression of gravity in keeping with his own and suitable to the revelation of so black a piece of news.

"General Clarke is the only one for this island," said the commander. "The others are going elsewhere. As you probably know, the Navy is to have full charge here, eventually; but for the present . . ."

He left the sentence unfinished. The implication I gathered was that, for the present, Commander Brigham and what other Navy men were aboard were to suffer the unspeakable humiliation of being under Army authority.

We went up to the bridge deck where General Clarke had his cabin adjoining that of the ship's captain. He was sitting on the edge of his bunk lacing up his shoes as we entered at his loud "Come in! Come in!" in response to our knock.

"Colonel, how are you?" he roared heartily, even before Commander Brigham had the chance to introduce me. "I can tell National Guardsmen far as I can see 'em," he added, with a grin. "Expectin' us, wasn't you?"

"Yes," I replied, "but not in this ship."

"I know. Change of plan at the last minute. This old

floating incubator's got chickens for more than one market. Got to work fast these days, Colonel. Got to improvise. Plans made in the morning blown up three or four sizes before night. Got a mixed grill aboard here: Army, Navy, even a job lot of civilians. All we lacked was a representative of the National Guard. . . . Sit down, Commander! Sit down! Hell's fire! Make yourself at home!"

There was an expression of iced suffering on Commander Brigham's face. However, he accepted the invitation. The general went on: —

"You see, Colonel, it's like this: I wasn't supposed to come out here. Last-minute appointment you might say. The Navy got such hell knocked out of 'em at Pearl Harbor that all the spare admirals and vice-admirals been put on fatigue duty over there, cleanin' up the mess. So the Gov'ment had to call on the old, dependable, ever-ready Army. We got to pinch hit for 'em till the Navy gets over the jitters and pull theirselves together a bit. That right, Commander?"

Plainly, Commander Brigham was not temperamentally equipped to defend himself against a leg-puller. Respect for superior rank, even though it *was* Army, may have prevented him from making any reply to this sally.

"You mustn't mind me," said Clarke, with a grin. "When you come right down to it, I guess the Army's got about as much reason to feel sick over Pearl Harbor as the Navy has. If we'd both been on the job December seventh there'd have been no need for bases way out in this part of the Pacific. Maybe they won't be needed anyway. Hope not.

"But here we are," he added, brusquely, "and this is no time to be saying 'if.' . . . Now, Colonel, what's the layout ashore?"

I made a brief report of the situation there, speaking of the examination I'd made of the atoll and of the map prepared, containing my suggestions. I said nothing at the moment of Father Vincent or the Lehmanns.

"Good," said the general. "I'm no engineer. Leave all that part of the business to you two. Quicker it's done the better." He glanced at the calendar hanging over the table by the side of his bunk. "This is Sunday, and my brother generals aboard — one of 'em outranks me, Commander — say their men need a run ashore. Been cooped up here ever since San Francisco and they've got a long way to go yet. It's only fair to give 'em the chance."

"How many are going on?" I asked.

"Four hundred. There's a hundred and eighty in our detachment, but we'll keep them busy aboard ship for today. Plan is to give the others a couple of hours' shore leave, two hundred at a time. That'll get the kinks out of their legs, anyway. Meanwhile, we'll start unloading our own gear so's to be ready for work the minute the ship leaves. How long do you reckon that'll take, Commander?"

"Is there a wharf here?" Brigham asked.

I explained that there was a solid coral-slab jetty that would serve for unloading the small gear, but that it was too narrow for the tractors, graders, and the other heavy equipment. "But there's good depth for the ship all along the beach at a distance of thirty yards," I added.

"That's easy then," said the commander. "We'll run across a temporary unloading stage. . . . We can have nearly everything ashore by nightfall. An hour or two in the morning will, certainly, see the end of it."

"Fine!" said the general. "Now I'll have a bite of breakfast and see you on deck in ten minutes."

I was rapidly becoming George P. Dodd of Detroit once more. The freighter had brought the U.S.A. climate along with the other supplies, and as I breathed the energy-charged air, the old feeling of nervous tension, the old desire to "fill the unforgiving minute with sixty seconds' worth of distance run" returned as strongly as ever. Furthermore, I wanted to get my part of the job done with so that I could leave at the earliest possible moment.

As the commander and I went out on the bridge, Viggo was standing by the captain, conning the ship around the coral shoals between the lagoon entrance and the village.

"Those coral heads will have to be blasted out one of the first things we do," said the commander. He had expressed, almost word for word, my own thought on the morning of my arrival in the schooner. He then left me to give his orders for starting work on the unloading stage.

The American climate had had no effect upon Viggo, insofar as I could see. His moment of excitement, after the ship was sighted, had vanished and he was his tranquil self once more. You would have said that he had been accustomed all his life to piloting ships into Low Island lagoons. I could see, from the relaxed expression on the captain's face, that he had complete confidence in the pilot.

The ship was not then brought up to the pier but anchored one hundred and fifty yards off the beach. Meanwhile, General Clarke came up, and as soon as Viggo was free I introduced him. The general cottoned to him on first sight and called him "Viggo" from the start, as, in fact, everyone did. Viggo had the faculty of appearing in the guise of an old friend upon five minutes' acquaintance. This was owing, I think, to his innate goodness, to the honesty and decency upon which his character was based. You knew at once where you stood with him.

All the village had gathered on the beach on either side of the pier. They were dressed in Sunday garb, the men in white shirts and trousers, the old women in flowing Mother Hubbards, the younger ones in their best flowered muslins. All were barefoot. There wasn't a pair of shoes amongst the lot.

"Quite a little family you've got here, Viggo," said the general. "How many are there?"

"One hundred and ten," said Viggo. "No . . . one hundred and eleven. There was a baby born last week. . . . What's the name of this ship?"

"*Pioneer*. . . . Why?"

"The parents of the baby want to give him the same name."

"Not a bad name for a baby at that," said the general.

"They'll have a hard time pronouncing it, though," said Viggo.

However, they managed it in the peculiar native fashion of pronouncing words and names strange to them. I learned later that the baby was called Pioniri, shortened, for convenience, to Pio. The letter *i* in their speech is pronounced like our long *e*.

"They thought the ship would be coming right up to the wharf," said Viggo. "They've got a kind of a song of welcome they want to sing. Shall I tell them to go on with it?"

"Sure, go ahead," said the general.

Viggo waved his hat toward them with repeated arm's-length gestures, and a moment later the chorus burst into song. Unfortunately, the breeze was blowing onshore so that the full effect was lost; and the noise on board, with the winches going, interfered with it still more. A big launch was being lowered over the side, and, following that, a flat-bottomed barge.

The general stood with his head turned sidewise, his hand cupped around his ear.

"Kind of funny singin', ain't it?" he said.

"Do you like it?" Viggo asked.

"Can't tell whether I do or not with all this racket goin' on. . . . Now, Viggo, we got to work fast here, as Colonel Dodd's probably told you. Captain wants to get his ship away first thing tomorrow morning. Biggest part of this outfit's going on, you know. Want to give the men of that part a run ashore. Be all right, won't it?"

"Yes, of course," said Viggo.

"Good! Start 'em going right away. Meanwhile, I want to have a look at the place across the lagoon the colonel told me about. Have to shift the people over there quick so's we can start work.

"You mean you want to go this morning?"

"Sure. How far is it?"

"Eight miles, but it's dead to windward the way the breeze is blowing this morning. We'll have to beat up to it, General. It will take quite a while."

"You needn't worry about that. We're not going in one of your canoes. Take a launch. Be over there in half an hour. . . . Where's Commander Brigham? He'll want to come with us."

Another launch had been put into the water by this time and brought to the foot of the ladder on the off side of the ship. Meanwhile, the big launch, crowded with shoregoers, had put off from the opposite side.

In a kind of daze, Viggo climbed down the ladder with the general, Commander Brigham, and me, into the smart Navy launch with its smoothly purring engine, waiting for us.

"Now where away?" said the general.

Viggo pointed out the distant *motu* where the tops of the coconut palms made a faint blur on the horizon.

"There's deep water all the way across," he said.

"Then open her up, young man," said the general. The launch gathered speed, throwing up clouds of spray as it hit the cross seas.

"She certainly goes, don't she?" Viggo exclaimed, admiringly.

"Fine lagoon you've got here," said the general. "Deep water like this everywhere?"

"Pretty near everywhere after you get offshore, except for the shoals near the passage."

"Viggo, we're all prepared to take care of the people here," said the general. "Feed 'em and everything."

"Oh, there'll be no need for that," said Viggo.

"That's all right. Gov'ment orders. Got to see that they're all right. That's why I want to have a look at the place they'll have to shift to. Put a warehouse up there to hold supplies for 'em. What do they live on, mostly?"

"Well, there's coconuts . . . and fish . . ."

"Mean to say that's all they have to eat? Coconuts and fish?"

"That's the main part," said Viggo. "We raise some pigs and chickens. We get supplies from outside, too: a little rice and flour and tinned beef. Of course, that's pretty well stopped since the war."

"How often do you have boats here?"

"There's a schooner comes twice a year on the average," said Viggo.

"Twice a *year!*" exclaimed the general. He shook his head, incredulously. "Young fellow," he added, turning to the boy steering the launch, "how'd you like to live on an island where you had a boat twice a year?"

"I think I'd like it, sir, for a while, anyway."

"Well, here you are! Here we all are. Guess we're going to like it whether we like it or not. But the schooner twice a year is out. You're on the map from now on, Viggo — the Army and Navy map, anyway. Even got a new name for you."

"What is it?" Viggo asked.

The general shook his head.

"That's a secret. . . . Call it 'P-R-B 9' if you want to — Pacific Reserve Base Nine. That would be something like it. . . . Where you from?" he asked, turning once more to the steersman.

"Kansas, sir."

"Where you other boys from?"

The launch had a crew of three. One was an Iowa boy and the third from Nebraska.

"It beats all how you fellers from the Middle West flock into the Navy," said the general. "Ignorance, I suppose. You don't know what you're lettin' yourselves in for."

All three grinned.

"We're learning fast, sir," one of them said. "I can't say I'd change to the Army if the chance was offered."

"There you are," said the general, "gettin' the Navy spirit before you've been in service a year!"

"Two years, sir, in my case."

"Then you're lost," said the general, his eyes twinkling. "We might have saved you if it'd been only a year. But two years . . . you're done for! That right, Commander?"

Commander Brigham made a faint attempt at a smile, but it struck me that he didn't at all approve of the general's chaffing with the crew of a Navy launch.

We were fast approaching the *motu*. As I've said, this particular one was about a quarter of a mile long, the largest on this far reef of the atoll. Viggo had told me that it was the custom of the natives to move over here in a body twice yearly to collect the coconuts from all the islets along this side. The nuts were opened and the copra dried here. It was a kind of communal picnic for the entire population and made a pleasant break in the tempo of their lives. A village of small shelters would spring up overnight. The men fished and loafed while the copra was drying. The women and children gathered up the fallen fronds and tidied the *motu* from end to end. They also engaged in the particular kind of fancywork common to the women of the atolls. On this *motu* were found great quantities of tiny, multicolored shells from which they made necklaces, hatbands, and other ornaments. They were beautifully designed, with a shading and arrangement of various colors and sizes that made them works of art.

But now as we approached, the *motu* had the appearance of being one never before seen by the eyes of man. The long smooth beaches were untrodden, marked only with the shadows of the trees that shaded them. I could see from the expressions on the faces of the boys from my own part of the U.S.A. that this was a memorable experience for them, just as it had been for me. I wondered whether any of them, in grammar school, had examined, in their geographies, a sketch with the caption, "Atoll — a Coral Island," printed beneath it. Probably not. School geographies in these days are illustrated by photographs, I believe. There is a world of difference between a photograph of an atoll and a sketch made by someone who had only dreamed of such places: someone short on exact knowledge, perhaps, but long on the strangeness and mystery and beauty of the imaginative conception. Even the sketch falls far short of the reality in these very qualities. I was sorry for the boys whose duty required them to remain with the launch. This was their first, and it might be their only, chance to see a Low Island *motu* in its natural condition, before the impending change was under way.

There was no sentiment in General Clarke, and I

liked him none the less for that. He didn't appear even to notice the sea fowl, the strange vines and plants, the shadows on the sand, or the vistas through the trees of the surf piling in over the outer reef. He was all intent on the job in hand. He halted when we had reached the upper slope of the beach.

"Wouldn't be a bad place for the storehouse right where we are," he said. "What do you think, Commander? Unless Colonel Dodd's found a better one?"

The commander agreed, and I said that it was the place I had fixed upon and marked, tentatively, on my map.

"Good! That's settled, then. Wish everything could be settled as easy. . . . Now that we're away from the boys, Viggo, I want to speak of the toughest problem of all. I guess you know what that is?"

"No . . . I can't say I do, General."

"Hmmm! You never been in the Army, that's sure. *Or* the Navy. You've never had to keep a fatherly eye on a lot of young bucks such as I've got here. It beats all how, the minute they've got time for something beside their duties, they all pick the same something to think about."

"Oh," said Viggo; "you mean . . . women?"

"That's it. We're not so old ourselves but what we can remember how it was with us at twenty or around there. . . . How many young women are there in the village?"

"Around twenty-five. Maybe a few more; that is, young women. But General, they couldn't . . ."

"Wait a minute, wait a minute, Viggo! I'm not hintin' that I want you to recruit a corps of concubines for this detachment. Cost the Gov'ment too much payin' 'em overtime. No, no! I'm thinkin' of the girls and how to keep 'em out-of-bounds to a hundred and eighty young lustyguts, most of 'em in their early twenties."

"They're not all skirt-chasers, General," said the Commander.

"Hell, Commander! Don't suppose for a minute I'm thinkin' of your Navy boys. Everybody knows from observation that not a gob in ten thousand would look at a skirt unless he was ordered to. No, no! The girls are safe from the Navy, but I'm worried about the rest of the outfit."

The commander smiled at this, the first encouragement I'd had that he might improve upon better acquaintance.

"Joking aside, I want to get your people over here as soon as possible, Viggo. The commander's right in what he said just now. We've got a fine lot of fellows in this outfit. There'll be no trouble at all with the greater part of 'em. They'll sit of an evening and look at their girls' pictures. They'll remember the promises they made before they left home . . . and keep 'em, too, since they'll have no chance to break 'em. I watched and studied 'em pretty careful on the voyage. To make a rough guess, I'd say not more than half have women-on-the-brain right round the clock, and some of them are okay, otherwise. The rest have got the disease only from around 6 P.M. till Lights Out, or a little later when they can't go to sleep. We're going to work 'em so hard on this job that Lights Out will *mean* sleep; at least, till we've got things all shipshape here."

We walked across the *motu* and back and Viggo took the occasion to speak of the water situation.

"We've got no reservoir over here," he said. "The people can use green coconuts for drinking to start with but . . ."

"There'll be no trouble about that," said the general. "There's a distillation unit we can set up here. Give 'em a steady supply all the time. . . . Colonel, you picked the right place for the population."

"It's the only place large enough to pick," I replied.

He nodded.

"And eight miles between them and us. Eight miles over, eight miles back. Guess none of the young fellers will want to swim that distance however anxious they are to go sparkin' the girls. But you must keep all your boats and canoes on this side, Viggo."

As we were walking down to the launch, he added: "Damned shame, ain't it? Hard on the boys, stuck way off in a place like this. They'll think war's just what Sherman said it was, even on a South Sea island."

The general invited Viggo and me to lunch aboard ship. It was only midmorning when we returned so we went ashore to change into less mussy clothing. As we approached the jetty we met the big launch returning with a crowd of the first detachment of shoregoers. While I was looking at them Viggo was gazing with astonishment at the work in progress on the unloading stage.

"Mr. Dodd, I wouldn't have believed this if I hadn't seen it! They've got it almost finished!"

"These jobs go in a hurry when you have all the materials on hand," I remarked.

"And it's to be only a temporary wharf?"

"Yes. We'll widen the jetty in a day or two. Make a good solid job of it. How long did it take you to build that pier?"

"Let's see," said Viggo. . . . "It was a little over eight months from the day we started till we got it finished. Of course, we didn't work at it all the time. There was no special hurry."

The scene on the beach was an animated one, to say the least: the shoregoers were trying to crowd all the enjoyment possible into the brief time granted them for stretching their legs.

"You don't know how strange all this looks to me," said Viggo. "They're well-behaved boys, aren't they? I guess it's as strange to them as it is to us."

Some of them, with the national passion for collecting souvenirs and mementos, were gathered in groups before the houses of the natives, trying to converse in sign language. One old woman who had just been visited was standing on her doorstep, both hands full of bills, gazing at them with an air of utter bewilderment. Spying Viggo, she beckoned to him earnestly and thrust the money into his hands, talking thirteen to the dozen.

"Mr. Dodd, will you look at this!" Viggo exclaimed when he had counted the money. "These boys millionaires? She's got sixty-four dollars here! It's what they gave her for a lot of shell wreaths and necklaces she had!"

"She makes the prettiest ones in the village, Viggo," I said.

"I know, but sixty-four *dollars!*" He gave me a blank look, shaking his head gravely. "The people here know next to nothing about money. Looks to me as if these boys don't either, throwing it away like that."

"Men in service are well paid nowadays," I said. "They've got so much it burns holes in their pockets."

Arriving at Viggo's house, we found half a dozen young Americans seated on the veranda enjoying the hospitality of Mrs. Viggo and their three daughters, Paki, Mona, and Thurid. The latter most resembled her father, the reason, doubtless, why he had given her the old Scandinavian name, Thurid, which the natives made pronounceable by calling her "Turi." She had beautiful copper-colored hair that made an aureole around her head in the sunlight. While none of the girls were what would be called handsome, they were very pictures of health and youthful vigor, with the fine easy carriage common amongst Polynesian women. The boys seemed to find them very agreeable to look at, and one of them could scarcely keep his eyes off Turi.

Viggo gave them a cordial welcome. Although none of his family spoke English, that seemed to matter little. They had made their guests feel at home, and brought them drinking coconuts which the boys were tasting with evident relish.

"I hope you don't think we barged in here, sir," one of them remarked. "Your wife invited us; at least that's what we understood."

"Of course she did!" said Viggo, heartily. "Wish we had room for all of you. It's too bad you boys have to go on so soon."

"I don't," said one, a well-set-up lad with hair almost as blond as Viggo's. "I'm with the detachment that's staying."

"Oh," said Viggo. "I thought none of you were given shore leave today."

The young fellow smiled, a bit guiltily.

"That's right," he said. "I came anyway."

"Shouldn't have done that, should you?"

"No, sir, but I couldn't wait. This is the first time I've ever seen a South Sea island."

"Maybe you'll have more than enough of this one before you've been here long."

"No, sir; not me. I was made for this kind of life."

"Don't be too sure," said Viggo. "A lot of you may think that at first. You'll probably be sick of the place two weeks from now."

"What of yourself, sir?" the boy asked. "You must have lived here a long time."

"I guess you've got me there," said Viggo, with a smile. "I'm kind of an old fool."

"And I'm a young one of the same kind," the other replied. He took up his coconut again, tilting back his head as he drained the cool refreshment to the last drop. "Boy! That's sure good! First time I knew what a coconut really was."

Viggo explained that these were the green nuts used for drinking. When the others had emptied theirs, one of the daughters split the nuts open with a heavy knife used for the purpose. Spoons were brought so that the guests could taste the creamy film of just-forming coconut meat inside. They did more than taste. They scraped the shells clean.

"That's what you might call a full meal," one of them said. "The meat to eat and the water to drink."

A moment later they rose, politely. "We'd better be going on, sir. We've only got two hours' leave. We want to see as much as we can."

They shook hands all round and I observed that the boy who was A.W.O.L. lingered over his farewell to Turi. They turned to wave again as they moved along the crowded village street.

"What fine boys!" said Viggo. "Will they all be like this, Mr. Dodd?"

"You mustn't expect too much," I replied. "There'll probably be all kinds just as there are in every army."

"Yes, of course. But I hope the ones to stop here will be mostly this kind."

We saw various kinds during the next hour. Having changed our clothing, we still had time for a leisurely stroll through the village before going out to the ship. The leave men were taking full advantage of the opportunity to stretch their legs. They had scattered in all directions over the *motu*. Some had brought bathing trunks and were swimming in the lagoon. Others visited Father Vincent's church, tip-toeing, caps in hand, up the aisles to examine the beautiful altar. Yet others were walking in his garden admiring the trees and shrubs and flowers. There were coconut-drinking parties all over the place. The native children went up the boles of the palms like so many monkeys to throw down green nuts, proud and happy to be of service.

The shyness of the young islanders was rapidly giving way to easy comradeship with the visitors. The American boys seemed to know by instinct how best to break the ice. They would point to this and that and the other, asking the native names, and the girls shouted with merriment at the attempts of the Americans to pronounce the names after them.

On the path near the spot where I had seen the sleeping children on the day of my arrival, a crowd had gathered around two expert harmonica players who furnished the music for two equally expert jitter-bug enthusiasts. Half a dozen of the girls were looking on with keen interest.

"Come on, sister! Have a try," one of the dancers said, seizing a girl by the hand. "Come on! I'll show you."

The girl understood his meaning very well, and after giggling and holding back for a minute or so, she stepped out with him. The harmonica players took a new lease on enthusiasm and seemed to be devouring their instruments. The other Americans grinned and shouted encouragement.

"Say! She's getting it! She's getting it! What do you know about that!"

"That's the ticket, sister!"

"Boy! She's got rhythm!"

"I'll say she has!"

The girl broke away laughing, and, with her hands over her face, ran back to the protection of her companions. There was a loud chorus of approval from the visitors, and as Viggo and I walked on they were urging the other girls to have a try.

"What in the world kind of dancing is that?" Viggo asked.

"It's what they call jitterbugging," I explained.

"Is that the way all the young people dance in America?"

"I wouldn't say all. But a lot of them do."

Viggo shook his head, glumly.

"My goodness!" he exclaimed. After a considerable silence he added: "And this is Sunday! I'm glad Father Vincent's not here!"

Another silence followed. He gave me a sidewise glance and then remarked: "I've never seen such a crazy dance . . . but she kind of got the hang of it, didn't she?"

Upon returning to the ship we found General Clarke waiting for us at the gangway. This easy informality was typical of him. He sent no orderlies to meet his guests and conduct them to his cabin, but did the meeting himself. Another thing about him that interested me was the pride he seemed to take in speaking English as though he had never seen the inside of a grammar school. He was, clearly, a man of breeding and education, but you would have said that he considered the fact a disgrace. His use of the mother tongue reminded me of the kind used by the professional Texans one hears in third-class radio programs. But sometimes he would forget that he was supposed to be "a regular guy," and his speech, while none the less salty and American, would be good Anglo-Saxon, and grammatically flawless.

"Boys havin' a good time ashore?" he asked.

"They certainly are," said Viggo.

"Behavin' theirselves?"

"Oh yes. If the men stopping here are like these, we'll be all right."

"They'll average up, Viggo. We've got a few hellraisers like I said, but sometimes men of that kind make better soldiers than the others."

We went to his cabin for a few minutes, then down to the dining saloon where the officers were gathering for lunch. We were introduced to the other two generals who stood somewhat on their dignity at first, but the mere presence of Clarke seemed to melt the stiffness out of them.

It gave me a comfortable, contented feeling to draw up to table in that company. There were men of all ages between twenty-five and fifty and not a weak or a crafty face amongst the lot. I tried to find a word to sum up the general impression, and "wholesome" popped into my head, followed by "dependable." They were the kind of men you like to rub shoulders with, the kind you would choose to stand back to back with in a tight place.

The lunch was excellent, and it did my heart good to see Viggo's enjoyment of the meal. I did full justice to it myself, and set my teeth into the best steak — in fact, the only one worth calling a steak — I'd enjoyed since leaving San Francisco.

The conversation was general throughout the meal, and I discovered that there was one subject, at least, in which the Army and Navy are in complete accord: the Japanese. The talk turned to those in the U.S.A. and the Hawaiian Islands, and what should be done with them after the war. Every man there believed in the advisability, but not in the probability, of their being sent back to Japan.

"It'll never be done," said General Clarke. "Wait and see. Take those on the West Coast, especially in

California. Them soft-headed, soft-handed native sons will let 'em come right back, soon as the war's won."

"Whoa, there, General!" someone called from down the table. "I'm one of those native sons."

"Excuse me, Major. I forgot," said Clarke, with a grin. "But that's what you'll do. You Californians are too damned lazy to do your own offshore fishin' and to raise your own garden truck. My guess is that, six months after the war's over, the Japs will be right back at their old Golden State, Golden Opportunity snoopin' jobs."

"They're a problem, no question of that," another officer remarked. "The worst of it is that many of them are, probably, loyal U.S. citizens and there's no way of separating the bad from the good. But the greater problem is: how are we ever again to have even professedly friendly relations with the Japs in Japan, knowing what we now know about them?"

"'What we *now* know'?" said the General. "We've *always* known it; that is, everybody outside of Washington. So did Washington know, but they found it expedient to pretend they didn't. It was expedient to sell the Japs gas, and oil, and steel, and scrap, and planes, and anything they'd a mind to ask for, to be used in bombing hell out of the Chinese. But you can't blame it all on Gov'ment. Gov'ment and Business — there's the 'expedient' twins! When you think of all the dirt they've done China, under the guise of friendship, it's the world's wonder the Chinese haven't become our bitter enemies, long since."

"But General . . ."

"Wait, just a minute! Let me get this off my chest. Gentlemen, if that word 'expedient,' and all it stands for in international relations, ain't blotted out of the dictionaries they use in Foreign Offices and Departments of State, we'll never have a world that's worth a damn to honest men. Gov'ments have got to learn what individuals have always known: that clear-cut questions of right and wrong can't be settled by expedient methods. If a certain course is wrong and would compel you to break faith with sworn friends, you don't follow it. If another course is dead right, and the only one that *can* be followed with decency and honor, you go right down that street. You don't wait to be pushed or scared into it. You go of your own accord, no matter how inexpedient you may find it to do so. And you hold that course, come hell or high water!"

"Three cheers, General!"

Clarke grinned, apologetically.

"Excuse me," he said. "I get hot around the belly-band whenever I think of the way we've treated China. Guess it's because I served in the East. Gave me a chance to size up the Chinese alongside of them teeth-suckin' 'So-solly' boys. . . . Let's talk of something else."

After lunch the general went ashore with Viggo while Commander Brigham and I took the launch to examine the shoals near the passage. We planned to start blasting them out as soon as the ship left. We then crossed the lagoon, as the commander wished to see the islets along that far side. Among others, we visited Viggo's turtle refuge. I told the commander of my sojourn there and of Viggo's love for the place, hoping that what I said would soak in and the *motu* be left unoccupied. The commander didn't commit himself one way or the other.

We returned late in the afternoon to find the general on board again. From then until suppertime and for three hours thereafter we were busy in his cabin, with my map spread out on the table. Both the general and Commander Brigham fixed upon the *motu* where the Lehmanns lived as the ideal place for headquarters. No mention was made either of the Lehmanns or of Father Vincent. The commander knew nothing about them at this time, and I gathered that Viggo had not spoken of them to the general. I awaited a more suitable opportunity, when alone with him, to bring up the matter of the Lehmanns.

The commander left us at half-past ten, but not

to sleep. In fact, there could have been little sleep for anyone aboard ship until the small hours of the morning. The winches were going full tilt, as tractors, graders, rooters, angledozers, planes in crates, and other heavy gear were swung over the side and lowered to the newly made wharf.

Presently the general folded the map and pushed back his chair with a sigh of content.

"Colonel, let's call it a day," he said. "And a mighty good day it's been. We've got a lot done. . . . Any objections to a Scotch-and-soda?"

He rang for a messboy who returned with two tall glasses filmed with icy vapor. That highball looked good to me. It was the first I'd had since leaving San Francisco. The general told me that he rationed himself to one a day. "And I always wait till night to have it," he said. "Gives me something pleasant to look forward to."

He raised his glass. "Here's to P-R-B 9," he said. "That's a camouflage name, of course, one that we'll use here amongst ourselves. I can't give even you the real one."

He sipped with gusto and set his glass down carefully.

"It's a damned shame about that old priest," he said. "What's his name? Father Vincent?"

"Oh . . . Viggo told you about him?"

"Yes. . . . I saw his church and garden. Hate to think all that's got to be wiped out."

"I feel the same way about it," I replied.

"If only they were somewhere else! . . . But wishing won't move 'em, and there they are, right in the middle of what will be the landing field. . . . The blasted war! Who'd have thought, a few years ago, that these bits of islands would ever be involved in one? It's going to be as hard on the natives as on the old father. . . . Hell!"

"Did Viggo speak of the Lehmanns?" I asked.

"The Lehmanns? No. Who are they?"

"They live on the islet across the passage: a father and daughter; Jewish refugees who came to the island eight months ago."

"Christ A'mighty! Have we got a Jewish problem to deal with way out here?"

"No, not a problem," I said. "An asset, and a valuable one, in my opinion."

I went on to tell him, briefly, what I had learned of the history of the Lehmanns and what I had gathered from my own observation. I spoke of Miss Lehmann's stenographic abilities and of the fine musical talents of both father and daughter. I suggested that two such persons could perform a valuable service here, amongst young men who, when their day's work was done, would have little to do and no place to go. In fact, I believe I became a bit eloquent in presenting a case for the Lehmanns. The general heard me through in silence; then he said: —

"Colonel, it's impossible. It's simply out of the question. My orders are that no one outside the Service is to be permitted to visit the island, to say nothing of living on it. The only exceptions are the resident agent and any missionaries established here, which lets in Viggo and the old priest. I'm truly sorry. I have deep sympathy for all refugees, Jewish or otherwise, but you see how I am fixed? Orders are orders. The Lehmanns will have to go."

"Yes, I see that," I replied.

"If the decision rested with me . . . But it doesn't. And that's that. . . . Let's see what's going on."

We went out to the port side of the bridge deck and stood for a while watching the work in progress below us. The ship lay moored with her bow alongside the coral jetty and her stern at the unloading stage. The heavy equipment was now ashore and other supplies were coming out the hatches both fore and aft. The intense light from the cargo clusters, mingled with that of the waning moon, lit up the scene with a bizarre, unreal effect. It was now well past midnight, but many of the natives were still on the beach or looking on from a distance, amongst the groves. The moon had lost none of her old serenity, but the waning light, I thought, might have been that of a last appearance. And, certainly, she would not, for years to come, if ever, look down again on the old peaceful island it had been my privilege to see for so brief a time. Before the coming of the next full moon, that island would have ceased to exist, and P-R-B 9 would be in its place.

The general's reflections were running in a direction similar to my own.

"The cursed Huns!" he exclaimed, bitterly. "What haven't they to answer for? I wonder if there is anyone, anywhere in the world, whose life has not been at least partly ruined by their beastliness?"

"I wouldn't give all the credit to the Huns of Hitler's *Reich*," I replied. "Some must be saved for their blood brothers in Tokyo."

"You know, Colonel, there ought to be a new word coined to include both tribes in the same breath. . . . But where, from the depths of Evil, could the ingredients for a fitting word be dredged up? . . . Well, I'm going to turn in. We can really get going tomorrow."

I found Viggo on the beach. He had, evidently, been waiting for me. We walked to his bench on the opposite side of the *motu* where we had before us the expanse of moonlit sea, unbroken to the horizon line. It seemed to be slightly uptilted toward the land, as though the island lay in a shallow depression, in the center of a brimming silver bowl.

"I didn't mention the Lehmanns to the general," Viggo said, presently.

"I know. . . . I've told him."

"And . . . they can't stay?"

"No."

"It's what I was afraid of."

"He has no choice in the matter," I said. "No foreigners save you and Father Vincent can be permitted to stay. . . . 'Foreigners'! That's a strange way of putting it! As though you and the father belong in that class!"

"I understand what you mean," said Viggo.

"I wonder if they're still up," I said. "I want to tell them at the earliest possible moment and get it over with."

"They haven't been over here today," said Viggo. "I walked along the beach by the passage a little while ago. I could see their light through the trees."

He volunteered to go with me, so we took one of the small canoes to cross the passage. The lamp with its shade of clouded, cream-colored glass was throwing out its mellow light from the end of the veranda where the piano stood; and even before we saw the light we heard music. Mr. Lehmann was playing something I have always loved, Raff's "Cavatina," to his daughter's accompaniment. Viggo and I waited below, in the shadows, until the playing ceased.

I'm sure that Miss Lehmann knew, the moment she saw us, what we had come to say. I didn't beat about the bush but told them at once.

They took the blow quietly as I knew they would, but that didn't seem to make the telling any easier.

"We have had eight very happy months here," Mr. Lehmann said, in his broken English. "We will never forget them. This time has been a great blessing for us. Now we are ready for anything."

"Father and I have really felt guilty, Mr. Dodd, being so . . . so safe and useless, in times like these. It has been the only thing to mar our happiness. Now we must try and find work that may help others a little, even if only a little."

I don't believe that I have a heart particularly susceptible to being wrung. But as I looked at these two fine people, as I tried to realize the full depth of the tragedy of their lives, I seemed to feel of a sudden the appalling weight of the burden of millions of other lives, wrecked as theirs had been. Here was grief too deep for human expression — a dry-eyed grief that seemed as fathomless as the Coal-Sack pit in the Milky Way.

Old Papa Viggo was thinking only of the Lehmanns and of what this news meant to them, and the tears trickled unchecked down his ruddy cheeks. He drew out his handkerchief, unashamed, and wiped them away.

"Ruth," he said, "it doesn't seem fair that you and your father . . ."

He couldn't get on with what he wanted to say. Miss Lehmann went quickly to him, leaned over the back of his chair, putting her cheek to his and her arms around his shoulders.

"Viggo, you good old friend! Why, this is nothing to feel so sad about!"

"But . . . we'll miss you here. . . . We'll all miss you. . . . And I don't see just . . . where you'll go now."

"Where? Why, to the other island, of course: the seat of government. That's not so far away. Father and I feel certain we can find something to do there."

"Well I . . . hope you can, Ruth. I . . . certainly hope you can!"

We didn't stay long, and we had nothing to say to each other as we paddled back to the village. Everything was silent there. Work had stopped and the peace of mid-ocean was flowing in again, seeming to widen and deepen from moment to moment.

"Do you suppose they've finished unloading?" Viggo asked.

"Yes; at least all the main part of the cargo," I replied. "There may be a little left to put ashore in the morning."

"It's morning now," said Viggo. "Must be two o'clock. . . . Well, good night, Mr. Dodd. I expect you're as ready for bed as I am."

"I'm going soon," I replied. "I want to have a look round for a bit to see how they've got things sorted."

I've spoken of the open space near Viggo's house where the *himiné* was held. It was a village common, used for all kinds of community purposes. The heavy engineering equipment had been brought to this place and ranged on either side: tractors, graders, shovels, bulldozers, rooters, and the like. I saw that nothing had been forgotten; in fact, the amount of equipment exceeded the need we would have for it; but the ship, or another one, was to call later to carry it all elsewhere.

I'd seen apparatus of this kind times enough in the past, of course, without thinking much about it one way or another, except from the engineering point of view. But as I looked at this double row of machines facing each other in the moonlight from across the little common, I had a feeling of apprehension, as though a corps of robots might emerge from the shadows to begin the work of destruction even as I looked at them. Of all the grotesque, incongruous, horrible sights, you would have to go far to find one to cap this of the machines, brooding in the moonlight on a coral island. I thought of the tens and hundreds of thousands of other machines scattered far and wide over the earth, thus brooding through the night, dreaming their fearful dreams, and, with man's help, making them come true.

VIII

THE WINCHES WERE SET going again at the crack of dawn and an hour later the last of our share of the cargo was ashore. The men of General Clarke's detachment then came off with their duffelbags and other personal gear. I noticed that several of them carried musical instruments. One had a piano accordion slung over his shoulder, two others carried violin cases, and there must have been half a dozen saxophones in the outfit. All these belongings were stacked for the present in a shed used for drying copra. The men then stood by to await orders, and once more the village was thronged with people as it had been on the previous day.

Great heaps of drinking coconuts had been assembled on the wharf as a gift from the islanders to the men who were going on. Much of the work of collecting them had been done the afternoon before, under Viggo's direction, and while the ship was preparing to unmoor, the nuts, thousands of them, were taken aboard in cargo slings and heaped on the forward deck.

The natives were still dazed and excited by the

events of the past twenty-four hours. When island people, whose lives have flowed tranquilly on in the same channel generation after generation for centuries together, are suddenly swept from their old bearings into a whirlpool of strange and incomprehensible events, time is needed for them to come to even a dim realization of their significance. As I strolled here and there during this hour of confusion before the departure of the freighter, I tried to put myself inside the skin of an islander, to imagine what he was thinking and feeling at the moment. Viggo was with me a part of this time, and I got an inkling of the situation through what he told me.

"They just don't know what's happening," he said, with a sad shake of the head. "And I don't see how I'm going to make them understand. Will you believe it? Some think the ship is leaking and that all this cargo has been put ashore so they can get at the leak. Others believe they've run out of fresh water and that's why we've given them the drinking nuts."

While we were talking, the old woman who had been given the sixty-four dollars for her shell ornaments came hurrying up to Viggo. I don't know whether or not she had been holding the money since the day before, but here she was again, and once more she thrust the bills into Viggo's hands, speaking in the same torrential fashion. She seemed to be pleading with him, and she became more and more earnest and entreating as he replied, with repeated shakes of the head. At last he seized her hand, placed the money in it, closed her fingers over it and gave her a gentle push, whereupon she went sorrowfully away.

"She wants me to buy her a sewing machine and a brass bed," Viggo explained, with a faint smile. "She thinks they must have them aboard the ship. She can't get it through her head that this isn't a trading ship like Tihoti's schooner."

"Don't they all sleep on mats?" I asked. "Outside your own house, I haven't seen a bed in the village."

"Yes," said Viggo, "but there isn't an old woman in the place that don't covet a brass bed, for show. The young ones want mirrors, big ones with gilt frames."

Presently we spied General Clarke coming in our direction.

"We shan't be long now, Colonel," he said. "All set, you and the commander?"

"We're ready to start in as soon as the ship leaves," I replied.

"Okay. Go to it! How have you lined up things between you?"

"The commander wants to supervise blasting out the shoals. I'll get work under way ashore."

"I'm going out with you in the ship, Viggo," the general said. "Want to have a last word with General Grover. On the way back we'll have a look at the headquarters islet. You can introduce me to the Lehmanns. . . . Go right ahead with things, Colonel; you and the commander."

There were so many things to go ahead with at the same time that I hardly knew where to begin. I went over them in thought while the ship was unmooring and the men aboard were shouting good-byes to their friends on shore. One of the first jobs would be clearing ground for the barracks and the building to house the supplies, but before that work could be gotten under way the natives had to be shifted to the *motu* across the lagoon. At the moment they were all gathered along the beach watching the ship as it drew slowly away from the wharf. Many of them, no doubt, only now realized that the ship was actually leaving behind the stores piled high in all the available space along the foreshore.

Commander Brigham joined me as I was standing there.

"I'll get work at the coral heads started within the next half hour," he said. "Lieutenant Kelly is assembling the men of your shore unit. He'll be ready for orders as soon as you want to give them."

"Is he a Catholic?" I asked.

"I suppose so. Never knew a Kelly who wasn't. No objections to that, are there?"

"Not at all. On the contrary," I replied.

I had already met the lieutenant, a husky young fellow who, in peacetime, had been a foreman with a big West Coast construction company. All of his men belonged to an engineering company of the regular Army, although many of them had only recently joined the Service. They had changed to fatigue dress before leaving the ship.

One job, the destruction of Father Vincent's church, could be started immediately. I was bound that this should be done carefully, with all the reverence a work of destruction will permit. Lieutenant Kelly was the man to supervise it, and I learned that a good third of his detachment were Catholics.

"You can leave it to me, sir," he said. "I'll see that it's properly done." He shook his head, sadly. "But it'll be sorry work. Such a pretty little church! What will his Reverence say when he comes back?"

When I returned to the village an hour later, I found General Clarke and Viggo standing near the latter's house. The general was speaking earnestly as I came up.

"But we've got to clear 'em out," he was saying. "We can't get properly started till the natives are out of the way."

"I know," said Viggo, in his quiet apologetic manner; "but if you can give them a little more time? They don't understand yet what's happening. It's all come so quick they're still kind of dazed."

"Time! We've got no time to spare," the general replied, in an exasperated voice.

The natives were standing in the doorways of their thatched houses or wandering aimlessly here and there. The general scratched his head as he looked about him, and the hard-boiled expression on his face softened a little.

"It's a damned shame, having to root them out of their homes like this," he said. . . . "Listen, Viggo! Tell 'em it's not our fault. Tell 'em they've got them little yellow devils from Tokyo to blame for all this. And tell 'em that, before this war's over, Uncle Sam is going to make that so-called Rising Sun set so hard they'll feel the tidal wave from the splash way out here."

"I couldn't explain that, General," said Viggo. "They don't even know who the Japs are."

"What!" said the general. "Ain't you told 'em?"

"Yes," said Viggo; "Father Vincent and I have both spoken about the Japs, but they don't really understand."

The general turned to me with a give-it-up expression.

"Colonel, can you beat it?" he asked.

"I don't know that you can blame them," I replied, "when you remember how little we ourselves understood before Pearl Harbor."

"You've said it," the general replied, with a grim smile. "If we're going to talk about dumbness, I guess we'd better start right at home."

I don't know how Viggo managed it, but before midday the people understood that they were all to move and had started packing their belongings. There was no great amount to pack. Looking about me, I realized how few material possessions are needed for a comfortable and a happy life in a place like that. Each family had about the same articles: mats and pillows and a few handmade patchwork coverlets which they call *tifaifai;* a kettle or two and a large iron pot; a wooden chest for clothing; an *ana*, which is a wooden stool with a coconut grater attached, and the men's fishing spears. There were two or three sewing machines, which, doubtless, served the needs of all the women of the village. Except for these and the cooking utensils, their belongings were homemade. I did see a superb brass bed. I suppose it was that which had set the other women to longing for one like it — for show. Each family had the same one-volume library, a well-thumbed Bible, translated long ago into their dialect of the Maori speech.

LOST ISLAND

At noon our men knocked off for chow, and at this time tins of bully beef and salmon, with hard biscuits, were distributed to the natives. They certainly ate with relish. I was surprised, in a place where fresh fish are so plentiful, to see the gusto with which they tucked into the salmon. Viggo told me they considered it a great luxury. I suppose they liked the different taste of the canned fish.

As soon as the meal was over they set to work dismantling their dwellings. Once started, they worked with a will; I was astonished at the speed with which the huts came down. The plaited palm fronds were bound to the framework with lashings of sennit. This was of no value for they could easily plait new ones, but the framework of the houses they took carefully apart to set up again on the other *motu*. The islets being small, wood is a valuable commodity. Furthermore, the natives love their trees individually and hate to destroy one for housebuilding.

In an hour's time, the village, with the exception of Viggo's house, had vanished. Nothing remained but the bundles of posts and rafters, and the old thatch heaped up for burning. Viggo's house was to stand. He had to have a place to live and the plot of ground it occupied could easily be spared. For the present his wife was to stay here with him, but his daughters were to go to the other *motu* with one of Mrs. Viggo's brothers who would take them in with his own family.

Insofar as I could tell the natives felt no resentment toward us. Though they might well have been bitter and sullen, I neither saw nor heard anything to indicate such feelings on their part; but there was many a sad face amongst them. I noticed in particular one sweet-faced old grandmother seated on a coral-slab doorstep, all that remained of her dwelling, with her small possessions tied up in a bedquilt beside her. She gazed in dismay at what had been the village street, shaking her head sorrowfully and saying *"Aué! Aué!"* over and over again. This is a common expression amongst Polynesians. By various inflexions of the voice it may express surprise, compassion, regret, fear, joy, or grief. I had no doubt as to its meaning on this occasion.

Meanwhile, the youngsters, both boys and girls, had scattered over the *motu* to drive in their pigs and fowls which are allowed to run wild for the most part. That chase was something to see. Our men helped, or tried to, and in the excitement and fun of the quest, everyone forgot the sadness of the occasion. Low Island pigs beat any I've ever seen for intelligence and agility. They are small and wiry and can they run! They seemed to enjoy the chase even more than the pursuers. They would wait, alert and ready — with something you would swear was a grin on their faces

— while three or four of our men were slowly closing in upon them. Then, as a grab was made, they were away like greased lightning, leaving the hopeful chasers sprawling and clutching at empty air.

General Clarke laughed till the tears came; in fact, the lot of us, grownups and children, whites and natives, had a wonderful time, and the fun of it brought us all together on a common footing. I would give something to have a motion picture of that wild scramble, but I don't really need it. I've got it all in memory and my diaphragm quivers at the mere thought of it. Even Papa Viggo joined in. He thought he had one pig that was being driven straight toward him, with no apparent avenue of escape; but as he stooped to grab, the pig went between his legs as though shot from a catapult. As for the fowls, they were like partridges, swift and strong on the wing. By this time many of them were perched in the tops of the highest coconut palms, cackling in triumph, as though the nuts clustered in the nests of fronds beneath were eggs that they had laid.

"Viggo," said the general, wiping his eyes with the back of his hand; "I wouldn't have missed this for a thousand dollars!"

"They're kind of wild," Viggo said, apologetically.

"You don't need to tell me. I'd give odds on one of these pigs against a whippet any day. And if you could train the fowls like we train carrier pigeons, we wouldn't need our wireless. We could have hen-and-rooster communication between here and Honolulu."

It was thanks to the children that the greater part of the livestock was finally captured, and by that time it was midafternoon. A happy holiday spirit had seized the natives, like that, I suppose, of their semi-yearly migrations to the *motu* across the lagoon. Furthermore, not many of them could have realized as yet what would happen to their village islet before they saw it again. About thirty of them piled into our big all-purpose launch, and another thirty embarked with the community belongings in the flat-bottomed barge which was to be towed behind. The canoes, large and small, with the rest of the population, were taken in tow behind the barge, and presently the flotilla drew away from shore, the people singing and waving good-byes to the rest of us. Before they left I arranged, through Viggo, that twenty of the boys and young men should be sent for early next morning to strip the nuts from the palms. Our bulldozers and their drivers were protected by iron bars, one overhead and one to each side, against trees that might fall backward or sidewise against them, but they had not been built for coconut-grove destruction, and nuts falling from a height of from forty to sixty feet would be like salvos of dud bombs.

Viggo and I stood together, watching the flotilla until it was far out on the lagoon. He turned to me with a blank look.

"Old Kamaké!" he said. "I forgot all about him!"

"Would he want to go?" I asked.

Viggo shook his head.

"He's lived at the far end of the *motu* for at least thirty years. Couldn't we leave him there?"

"Yes, if he wants to stay," I replied. "But the old tree by his hut will have to come down. It would be right in the way of planes coming in to land."

"Well, I'll see him tomorrow," said Viggo, with a sigh. "I'll tell him about the tree, but I think he'll want to stay in any case."

The departing villagers were scarcely out of sight when Commander Brigham sent the small launch in to say that hundreds of dead and stunned fish were coming to the surface as a result of the blasting amongst the shoals.

"There's enough coming up, sir, to give ten times our whole outfit a feed of fresh fish," said the man who brought the news.

Little good the information did us with all the boats on the far side of the lagoon, and the Navy launch could not be used to cart fish ashore. I went with Viggo to the beach by the passage. A three-knot current was carrying the fish out to sea, and there were, literally, thousands of them, some still flopping feebly, but most of them unquestionably dead.

"It'll be a good feed for the sharks," said Viggo. "I certainly hate to see those shoals go. That was a fine place to fish."

With our portable generating units set up, work was continued in shifts far into the night, in the intense white glare of powerful lamps. In that distant part of the Pacific there was no present need for blackouts; nevertheless, the light was screened, on the seaward side, by means of tarpaulin curtains.

Father Vincent's church looked forlorn indeed as the general and I viewed it at nine o'clock that evening. The bell and belltower were gone; the roof had been removed and the framework supporting it. With the sheets of roofing iron, Lieutenant Kelly had built a temporary shelter on the ocean side of the *motu*. Here all the furnishings of the church — altar, stained-glass windows, benches, and the like — had been carefully stored. The timbers had been marked and numbered to simplify the task of rebuilding the church, should Father Vincent have the heart and the energy for the task. Nothing now remained but the empty shell, and that was fast disappearing. Men with pneumatic drills and sledge hammers knocked down the upper part of the walls, whereupon our bulldozers made short work of the bottom sections.

General Clarke sniffed the air, filled with the acrid stench from engine exhausts.

"Not much of the odor of sanctity left," he said, glumly. "It's a pity we're forced to do the kind of work the Huns are so fond of."

I'll not go into the details of the events of the following week. I was in a curious frame of mind during this time; in fact, I believe that most of us were, from the general down to the drivers of the tractors and graders. To some, no doubt, this destruction of a coral island meant little or nothing; it was merely the first part of an engineering job to be completed in the briefest possible time. You will find, on any such project, men who are thoroughgoing examples of the Industrial Age, and we had, I suppose, about the average quota in our detachment. To men of this kind, a swamp, green with wind-rippled rushes, refuge for all kinds of aquatic life, makes little appeal. It is something to be drained, filled in, and divided into factory sites or suburban real-estate projects. A fine asphalt-covered parking lot gives them more pleasure than the same acreage of meadowland, and they think of forests in terms of lumber or wood pulp. They have no more sentiment for organic life than the machines they drive. But it seemed to me that most of our outfit hated this work of destruction, particularly the early stages of it as we swept the *motu* all but clean of trees and bush. But once that was irrevocably done we could breathe more easily. The old island with its shady groves and paths was gone. Now it was an engineering project and we could get on with the work with interest and enthusiasm.

One's feeling about machines varies with the environment in which they are being used. For example, I'm down for a few days from the Alaska highway project. As you know, that colossal job is completed and the highway was formally opened by Secretary Stimson last November, but there's still plenty of work for engineers to do up there. Well, in such a wilderness, tens of thousands of square miles of virgin forest, mountains, and muskeeg, you have no doubt of the value of machines. There you see them as the friends and servants of man, giving him the power to conquer wild nature, seemingly hostile to his purposes, and to convert it to his own uses. But on a small coral island you are impressed not by the hostility of nature but by that of the machines themselves. You see their power from a different angle and have many a sober second thought as to the beneficence of that power.

As you know, the broad swath for the Alcan Highway, sixteen hundred and seventy-one miles of it, was cut through the Canadian and Alaskan wilderness in a single summer, sometimes at the rate of eight miles per day, and this against as formidable obstacles as men and machines have had to meet. Imagine, then, the simplicity of the task of making P-R-B 9. It was as though a djinn, with one short, contemptuous breath of mingled fuel-oil smoke and carbon-monoxide gas, had said, "Begone!" to the island that was. There was scarcely time to see it vanish.

During the moment, so to speak, of its disappearance, several vivid scenes were etched indelibly upon my memory. I watched the melting away of the knoll on the ocean side of the *motu:* Viggo's favorite observation spot; his "fine place to sit when you want to be alone." His bench and the two fine trees on either side would have been spared except for the fact that the knoll was wanted for filling in a depression crossing the islet from east to west that must have been made when the sea swept over the land in some great storm of the past.

Two bulldozers — Big Joe and Little Joe, the boys called them — with a rooter friend of theirs, were detailed for this work, and one could all but see their iron smiles as they approached the shaded, gently rounded knoll. "What!" they seemed to say. "Do they send *us* for this two-by-four job?" Big Joe coughed and sputtered his disgust. "Go on, Little Joe;

you take them trees. I'll stand by in case you need any help; but hell's fire! This is baby's work!" Little Joe jockeyed around them with the same air of contempt; then he went in, making deep and vicious bites at the roots and soil that held and fed them. About three minutes later Big Joe said: "All right, son. I'll take 'em now," and after a few powerful heaves and buttings, down they crashed, taking Viggo's bench with them.

As soon as they had been pushed out of the way friend rooter went to work, and in fifteen minutes' time the knoll was being carted away and dumped into the depression where the graders and rollers were busy. The boles of hundreds of coconut palms were neatly laid side by side in the depression, and on top of this went the knoll, together with the rubble that had been Father Vincent's church, his house, and the walls of his garden. Another of the vivid glimpses came when I saw a shovel — small as shovels go — scoop up what remained of the fifteen tons of High Island earth brought by the schooner and dump it into a truck. Then, as though looking around for more offenses against levelness, it seized upon a heap of coral sand and gravel not yet carted away and chucked that in on top.

Kamaké's tree went early the same morning. The work of clearing was started at both ends of the *motu*, and it went much faster than Viggo had believed possible. When he saw the speed with which trees were falling, he was in a hurry to warn Kamaké, so I took him in a jeep to that end of the *motu*. We arrived none too soon. Kamaké was seated near his hut, with several of our men standing around him, speaking loudly in an attempt to attract his attention.

"Hey, Grandpa! Come on, now! You'll have to shift out of here!"

They were relieved when Viggo and I appeared.

"He won't budge, sir," one of the boys said. "Is he deaf, or what? We were just about to pick him up and carry him away."

We stood at a little distance while Viggo spoke to the old man.

"He didn't pay no more attention than if we wasn't there," one of the tractor men said. "Guess he's a kind of an old dummy, ain't he?"

Perhaps I should have assembled the boys working in that vicinity and read to them the "Song of the Exalted Presence of Kiho-the-All-Source Concerning His Will to Bring Space and the Universe into Existence," but the moment was hardly a favorable one, so I replied with a mere nod of the head.

Viggo spoke with him for a moment or two; then Kamaké brought out his few belongings — the small chest, his sleeping mat, and the wooden headrest —

which he placed in his one-man canoe. He pushed the canoe into the water, climbed in, and paddled away in a northwesterly direction.

"Can you beat that!" one of the boys exclaimed. "I wouldn't have thought the old fossil had so much life in him."

That was my last sight of Kamaké. Viggo told me he was headed for a little *motu* seven miles distant.

"He'll be all right," he said. "He often goes over there to fish and stays for a week or two. But this time he knows he won't be coming back. . . . Kiho hasn't been very good to him, has he?" he added, with a bleak smile.

Ten days after the departure of the freighter, P-R-B 9 was a functioning unit in the United Nations far-flung defense and communication line across that part of the Pacific. At least, it was ready to function.

As I stood at the southeast end of the village *motu* it was hard to convince myself that I was on the same islet I had first seen such a little time before. From that vantage point there was now an uninterrupted view the full length of the *motu* to the burying ground at the far end. One had the impression of looking along the flight deck of an aircraft carrier; but the deck of this island carrier rooted to the ocean bed had been gently, almost imperceptibly, rounded to furnish perfect drainage in rainy weather. No tarmac runs were necessary, for our steam rollers had packed hard the crushed coral surfacing, making the entire landing field almost as smooth as the Lincoln Highway.

A double row of Quonset huts occupied the site of the old village, with Viggo's iron-roofed dwelling in the midst of them, like a bewildered old hen that has hatched a brood of chicks not at all what she had expected them to be. Prefabricated buildings of other kinds housed the stores, the mess hall, the hospital, the power plant, the machine and repair shops. The distillation unit carried a two-and-a-half-inch stream of fresh water into the underground tanks. Hangars for the land planes were sited along the ocean side of the *motu*, as far apart as possible. The mess hall for the enlisted men occupied part of the former village common. It was a combined mess hall, motion-picture theater, and general recreation room and could be quickly converted from one purpose to another. The radio station was located on a small *motu* half a mile distant along the reef to the southeast.

We left what trees we could, but they were woefully few. Those shading the beach where the village had been still stood, and a narrow ragged fringe remained along the ocean beach between the scattered hangars and the buried fuel-storage tanks. Camouflage of the base was an all but impossible task, but that was to be attempted shortly.

The only other job not yet completed was that on the *motu* across the passage. This, as I have said, was to be the headquarters islet, but General Clarke had delayed the work there on account of the Lehmanns. They were to go as soon as Tihoti's schooner returned. Viggo's house was used as temporary headquarters and his front veranda served as the officers' mess.

I'd seen nothing of the Lehmanns during this time, my days and nights having been fully occupied, but General Clarke had spent an evening, with Viggo and several other officers, in their company.

"Fine people, Colonel, first class," he had remarked upon his return from that visit. "You're right: they'd be a real asset here. Only trouble would be that every young feller in the detachment would fall in love with Miss Lehmann. I have myself, as far as that goes. Sang 'Annie Laurie' for me. Never heard it better sung. You'd say she'd been born and bred in Scotland."

As a result of that visit the Lehmanns were invited to attend a concert held several evenings later. Night work was now at an end and the men had asked permission to give an entertainment, a kind of housewarming, for the new mess hall. They were to furnish the talent and had appointed Lieutenant Kelly as their master of ceremonies. While we were having dinner that evening the lieutenant had suggested to General Clarke that the Lehmanns be asked to come.

"The boys have heard about them, sir. They thought they might be willing to help out with the musical part of the program. Maybe they'd let us bring the piano over."

"Good idea," said the general, heartily. "Go right ahead! If they'll come it will be a fine addition to the program."

No time was wasted. Immediately after dinner the lieutenant went across in the launch with a dozen of the boys and soon returned with the piano. The concert was to begin at half-past seven and well before that time every man not on duty came to the mess hall. Lieutenant Kelly brought the Lehmanns over. This was the first time most of the boys had seen them, and while the lieutenant was introducing them to the men taking part in the concert, others crowded round to be introduced. The general, Commander Brigham, Viggo, and I were sitting in one of the front rows.

"What did I tell you?" the general remarked. "She's takin' 'em by storm. She's the girl he left behind him to every young feller here."

That about hit off the situation, I thought. A part of Miss Lehmann's charm came from the fact that she was so unconscious of exerting it, and this was no affectation on her part. She was simple and natural and friendly without a trace of coquetry. Mr. Lehmann stood to one side, pleased and proud of the impression his daughter was making. Now that they had come there was to be a slight rearrangement in the program. Miss Lehmann was to play the accompaniment for the vocal numbers and both she and her father were to join the orchestra for some of the instrumental ones.

The boys were proud of their orchestra. It was top-heavy with saxophones, of course, but they had two violins — three with Mr. Lehmann — a flute, a clarinet, a piano accordion, and a bass fiddle. The opening number was the *Poet and Peasant* overture and it made the hit it always does. The boy with the piano accordion was an ace with that instrument, an orchestra in himself, and you would have said that the Lehmanns had played the *Poet and Peasant* times without number, which may have been the case. When it came to the pretty waltz refrain, Mr. Lehmann made his violin speak in a way that went straight to everyone's heart, and the boys playing with him outdid themselves in their pleasure at having a first-class violinist to lead them.

After that came all sorts of turns, musical and otherwise, but the one I remember best was a song that came toward the end of the program. The singer was a young aircraft mechanic with an excellent baritone voice, and by some miracle he was not a crooner. He first sang "When Day Is Done" to Miss Lehmann's accompaniment. There was tumultuous applause so he returned for an encore. As he placed the music before Miss Lehmann and she glanced over it, I saw a startled look come into her eyes. I don't think anyone else noticed it unless it was Viggo. Certainly, the young man didn't, but stood facing his audience, waiting for her to play the opening bars. The song was "You Will Remember Vienna."

You're probably familiar with the song; it's from a motion picture that was very popular some years back. There's real nostalgia in it for the old happy carefree Vienna; both words and music must have been written by someone who knew and loved that Vienna.

> As the years roll on
> After you have gone
> You will remember Vienna;
> Life that was happy and hearts that were free . . .

That's how the refrain goes, and every word must have been like a blow on the heart to the Lehmanns. But Miss Lehmann carried through her part like a Spartan. Not a tear did she shed.

There's little more to tell. Captain Tihoti's schooner returned the following day, bringing Father Vincent home. I'm not going into that. You will know how the old priest must have felt as he stood on the former village *motu*, gazing down the length of it toward the place where his church and garden had been. But he had a valiant spirit. I never saw him to better advantage than at that moment. The work of half his lifetime had been swept away, but you would never have guessed from his manner that the loss was of any great consequence. He was concerned only about his flock and how they were to live now, under the changed conditions. Within an hour of his return he was on his way to them.

I had been working on the *motu* to which they had been moved, installing their fresh-water distillation plant, and my heart was sore for every one of them. A few of them were halfheartedly plaiting palm fronds for their new houses, but for the most part they merely erected small lean-tos, temporary shelters, and let it go at that. They sat in groups or wandered aimlessly about the small islet, watching our men at work, but, seemingly, without the wish or the capacity for taking up the broken threads of their own way of living. I had the feeling that the coming of the freighter, with all that had entailed, marked the end of an era in Polynesian life, to be followed, perhaps, by changes even greater than those which had taken place when the ships of Wallis and Cook and Bougainville had first appeared over their horizons. And not only in Polynesia were these changes taking place. On islands and archipelagoes in the Western Pacific the patterns of native life were being broken up to a far greater extent. Perhaps, in the long run, it will prove to have been for their good. Who can say, now? Insofar as one small island of Polynesia is concerned I could see present evil very clearly, but I was not able to foresee the ultimate good to offset it.

Old Captain Tihoti was, I believe, hit harder by the changes than either Viggo or Father Vincent; at any rate, he showed it more. Viggo and I had lunch with him just before the schooner sailed, and he gave vent to his feelings in snorts, explosive sentences, and wrathful predictions of the fate of the island and its people, now that both had been drawn into the net of the Central Pacific defense line.

"It's done for," he said, bitterly. "Look at the place! What good will it ever be, again?"

Viggo tried to speak hopefully of the future, but the captain cut him short.

"Trying to fool yourself, Viggo," he said. "You know that as well as I do. What kind of a life can the people have now? Suppose the war lasts another two or three years — how you going to keep 'em cooped up on one little *motu*? They'll all die of boredom. Wait till they start flying the aeroplanes around here. What about the birds? Won't be any of 'em left in a few weeks. No, this island's finished. When the war's over it won't be worth a damn to anyone, white or native!"

We said good-bye to him and the Lehmanns the same afternoon. Since they had to go, the Lehmanns felt that the sooner they left the better, and the captain had no wish to remain a moment longer than was necessary. There was no lingering over the farewells. Miss Lehmann spoke quietly and cheerfully as though she and her father were going to an assured destination, but this, I could see, was largely for Papa Viggo's sake. All their possessions were in one small trunk and a suitcase, and Mr. Lehmann had his precious violin in its case under his arm. Viggo and I stood on the newly made wharf waving to them until the schooner was far down the lagoon heading for the passage to the open sea.

Orders for my own departure had already come. I had a new assignment, Alaska this time, and General Clarke informed me that I would be able to make at least a part of the homeward journey by air. A wireless message had been received of the coming of a plane, Honolulu bound from Australia via New Zealand. It was a four-motored transport plane and arrived the following morning. Captain Tihoti's prediction of what would happen to the sea fowl was borne out by the arrival of this first plane to land at P-R-B 9. It approached from the southwest and in circling the atoll it splashed through a cloud of birds hovering over one of the *motu* where the *kavekas* were then nesting. No harm was done to the plane except for the fact that it was spattered with blood and the mangled carcasses of birds churned to bits by the propellers.

There were some big shots on board, English, Dutch, and American, mostly civilian officials, part of the backwash that had followed the Jap invasion of Malaya, Java, and other places in the Western Pacific. All were U.S.A. bound, on various missions, I suppose.

We took off late in the afternoon and as we crossed the main islet at about five hundred feet, I had my last view of Viggo, waving a palm frond as he had that day on his turtle refuge, to scare the birds away. I wished him well with all my heart; but as I looked down upon that denuded island, swept bare of everything that had made it a pleasant homeland for its people, the desolation I felt was but a reflection of that which my eyes beheld.

I was to see the Lehmanns once more; at least, I was to see Captain George's schooner, carrying them on the next uncertain lap of a voyage that seemed destined never to end. They were far out at sea, and from our height of eight thousand feet the schooner looked no larger than half a matchstick. There was only a glimpse; then it was gone.

We passed ten or fifteen miles to the eastward of the island where I had landed from the plane on my voyage out. The sun had just set and the island stood out clearly silhouetted against the golden light. As I watched it receding swiftly behind us, I said, in thought, "Good-bye, Polynesia," with the fear in my heart that it was good-bye forever to the old peaceful life of those once remote islands and archipelagoes.

I was in a sober mood; perhaps my thoughts were gloomier than they should have been, but you must remember what I had seen happen to one of the islands in the space of three weeks. I felt, as I have said, that what was happening here was a tragedy for all mankind. For our planet is none too large, as many of us are beginning to realize, and if we give machines the scope they increasingly demand for their kind of life and activity, what kind of world shall we human beings have, in another half century? I had the feeling that, even before the war could end, the integrity of indigenous life, in no matter what remote corner of the world, might be so far destroyed that it would be lost forever.

I found these lines from the "Song of Kiho" running through my head: —

Now dreams the Almighty God.
Now the Almighty-God-of-the-Cosmic-Night dwelling below in Havaiki, visions: . . .
The unfolding of the wide realms of the Earth, a sanctuary for the living;
The under-propping of the Sky World here above, a Homeland for the Gods . . .

Where, I wondered, in days to come, would there be found any sanctuary for the living? As for the gods, the only one I was aware of in that ancient Polynesian homeland was the man-created, four-motored *deus ex machina* winging its way through falling night toward Honolulu.

IX

Webber was the first to speak.
"And that's the end?" he asked.

The engineer nodded.

"Of my part in the story," he replied. "As for what has happened since . . ."

They were silent for some time; then Professor Marsh said: "You will understand our interest, George. You've heard from your friend Viggo?"

"Yes, on several occasions."

"Well, then?"

"Phil, I've given you all the essentials. You can write the Epilogue for yourselves. As a homeland for its people the island has been destroyed almost as completely as Father Vincent's church and his garden. Let the broad statement suffice. Why dwell on the particulars?"

"Because you yourself did," Marsh replied. "And because, like yourself, I lack the detached, cosmic point of view. Human concerns are all-important to me, too."

"What ones chiefly, in this case?" Dodd asked.

"How is one to say, George? You've given me an ache in the heart from too many directions at once. While you were telling the story, I was thinking of the island in terms of some small community here at home, suddenly invaded and overwhelmed by forces that would be as strange, as unintelligible to us as ours to the Polynesians; and we as helpless against the invasion.... And yet, I'm not wholly sure that my first concern *is* for the natives themselves, except, of course, in a general way. You've not particularized them to any extent, as individuals..."

"I couldn't," said Dodd, "without making the story unconscionably long. And you must remember how brief a time I had to know them, and that I lacked their speech."

"I understand," said Marsh; "which is the reason, no doubt, why my concern goes out more strongly, perhaps, to Viggo, and the Lehmanns, and that fine old priest. What has happened in his case?"

"Wait, Phil," Webber put in. "Let that come in a moment. What about Viggo's turtles, and the sea birds? Did his refuge have to go?"

"Yes," said Dodd, "Viggo wrote me about that. The turtle refuge was taken over for gun emplacements, as I feared would happen. As for the sea birds ... I can tell you of them in terms of what happened on another lonely island, Ascension, where, as you may know, our Air Transport Service has established a base. I clipped this news item from a paper I was reading on the train, yesterday: —

"The difficulties of maintaining a base at Ascension have been due to its remoteness, its lack of any natural advantages, and its birds. Hundreds of thousands of sea birds stubbornly nested on the newly made runways. No matter how often they were shooed off, or splashed through by the huge air transports, back they came. The Army appealed to the ornithologists, who scratched their heads. Cats were imported, but the strong-winged boobies routed the cats. At last a curator of birds from the American Museum of Natural History made a special trip to Ascension. His uncomplicated solution was to destroy their eggs and to keep on destroying them till the birds gave up. For some time thereafter A.T.C. personnel ate eggs, walked on eggs, engaged in sham battles with eggs, with clouds of indignant 'wide-awakes' circling overhead. From the latest reports, the situation at Ascension, with respect to the sea birds, is now well in hand.

"That is how the problem was solved at P–R–B 9," Dodd added; "but I gather that no curator of dead birds from the Natural History Museum was needed to instruct them what to do."

"I can guess that another problem has not been solved so easily," Webber remarked, after a moment of silence. "What of General Clarke's hopeful plans for keeping his men apart from the island women?"

"You're right: they went all astray," Dodd replied, slowly. "As I've read Viggo's letters, I've felt that difficult situation becoming more and more acute. He has given me just enough anxious hints so that I was able to draw my own conclusions. But in his latest letter, without anything to prepare me for it, he announced, quite simply, that all three of his daughters are in the family way, by American soldiers."

Webber burst out laughing; then checked himself abruptly, gazing at the others in an abashed manner.

"Now why in the world did I do that?" he said.

Dodd smiled, faintly.

"It's understandable, Charlie. There is, often, something intrinsically comical in tragic situations. Perhaps it's the fullness of the measure, in Viggo's case, that struck you as laughable, here. The island he loved so much overrun by strangers and the life of its people completely disorganized; his turtle refuge gone, his birds gone, and now all three of his daughters — far gone in pregnancy. And no one really to blame, least of all General Clarke. He did his best, but he must have known, in his heart, what would happen. There are now three hundred and seventy men on the atoll, all of them young fellows, lonely, homesick, and, most of them, bored almost to death. Is it to be wondered at that they should seek distraction, consolation?"

"But . . . but how has this worked out, George?" Professor Marsh asked. "What of the island men? Does Viggo speak of them?"

"Yes. . . . Unfortunately, it hasn't worked out. It's not only the young women who are involved; the married ones, too. It's a forlorn situation; one of those problems without solution. In the case of one native husband — killed by a soldier, presumably in self-defense — there was stark tragedy."

"There must be scores of islands farther west in the Pacific where the same problem exists," said Webber.

"Undoubtedly . . . but there . . ."

"I was thinking," Dodd resumed, "of the far grimmer problem — of life itself — that the natives of those islands are faced with; of the fate in store for the vast archipelagoes in that part of the Pacific as the war gathers intensity. What will be left of their native inhabitants? What will be left of the islands themselves after hurricanes of shells, bombs, torpedoes, land and sea mines have laid them waste time after time? The desolation in Europe, Russia, North Africa, will not equal that of innumerable small islands subjected for months, perhaps years, to the concentrated destruction from both sides that is, certainly, coming. One can hope that Polynesia and the archipelagoes in the eastern Pacific have, at least, been spared that fate."

"Don't be too sure," said Webber. "There may be a World War III to come."

"I said that one can hope."

"What were those lines, George, in the Polynesian Song of Creation you read to us?" Marsh asked.

> "Erect at last, upon the Sacred Mound of My Temple,
> Ahu-Toru, Altar-of-Ascending-Fire,
>
> * * *
>
> "While the fire leaps upward in streaming flame.

"And now the fires are leaping again, but not the sacred fires of creation. . . . What would those so-called heathen think of our world of today, could they view it? And of us, the inheritors?"

"We might inquire of that old native," said Webber. "What was his name? Kamaké?"

"Yes," said Dodd. "He's still on the tiny *motu*, Viggo writes, the one he moved to when we started clearing the village islet. It's not more than twenty paces across, with a few old coconut palms and pandanus trees growing there. Fortunately, Kamaké has not had to be disturbed again."

"Now what of Father Vincent?" Marsh asked. "Does he plan to rebuild his church?"

Dodd shook his head.

"Viggo thinks not. I suppose that he hasn't the heart for it. I wish you could read Viggo's letters;

they are full of comment and sad speculation about Father Vincent and the Lehmanns. He writes just as he talks; I can feel the long periods of silence between the sentences. The old father, he says, carries on his work as quietly and faithfully as ever; but the disintegration of native life and the loss of his church and garden have been too much for him, at his age. Viggo writes that he often sees him standing on the old village *motu*, looking down the denuded land toward the place where his church and garden were, as though he cannot yet realize that they are irrevocably gone. The bell, the salvaged timbers, and the stained-glass windows remain where they were stored by the wrecking crew."

"What does he say of the Lehmanns?"

"Poor old Viggo! He worries as much about them as he does about Father Vincent. He's had only one letter from the Lehmanns, written shortly after their arrival at the other island, the seat of government. At that time they were expecting, or at least hoping, to find work there, but they gave him no details. For all their hope, he fears they may have had to go elsewhere. Now that the atoll is a military base, Captain Tihoti's schooner no longer calls there, so Viggo gets no more news through him."

Presently Dodd got to his feet and slowly paced the

room a time or two. Drawing a matchstick from his vest pocket, he broke it in half and tossed one piece onto the rug before him. Hands in pockets, he stood gazing down at it as though from a great height.

"You will remember my saying that, when I last saw Captain Tihoti's schooner, with the Lehmanns on board, the vessel was far out at sea, looking no larger than half a matchstick, from our height of eight thousand feet. I still think of the Lehmanns as being in that lonely, homeless, friendless situation, always forced to move on, like so many thousands of their race, to some unknown, uncertain destination. . . . If only wishing them well might help!

"There is another picture that comes often into mind," he added. "A picture of the island itself on a night of full moon. It was the night just before the freighter came, when I met Miss Lehmann in Father Vincent's garden and we walked together to the end of the village *motu*. She had said, 'It may be our last chance to see it as it is now,' and that proved to be the case. Having gone to the far point we walked slowly back, saying little, and when halfway to the village seated ourselves at the upper slope of the beach where we could look out over the lagoon. We had no further conversation; we merely sat there, enjoying the peace and beauty of the night, which seemed, somehow, beyond that of Earth. But at last Miss Lehmann broke the stillness to make a single perfect comment, a quoted phrase from Matthew Arnold's 'Rugby Chapel': —

". . . the moonlit solitudes mild
　　Of the midmost ocean . . .

"Just that — nothing more. A moment later we walked on, in silence, to the village."